As she bounced backward with a prolific apology, the wooden rails creaked. The last thing she needed to do was fall into the water with her tablet. She welcomed the strong pull around her waist, and she reached for the impeccably muscular arms.

"Whoa," the deep and now familiar voice said into her ear.

"Mr. Ravens." Zoe gasped. Once her eyes began to focus, she narrowed in on his lopsided smirk.

"Let's see, we've shared a plane, shared a seat on a plane, and I've walked in on you taking a shower."

Heat burned her cheeks. Zoe held her index finger up to correct him. "Almost in the shower."

Will inclined his head. "Okay, almost. However, I do believe we are beyond the formalities. Please call me Will."

Zoe bit the right corner of her bottom lip. "All right, Will. You'll have to call me Zoe."

"It's a pleasure, Zoe."

He had no idea what a pleasure it was to still be in his arms.

Dear Reader,

It's pageant season in Southwood, Georgia. Who doesn't want to be glitzed up by none other than renowned makeup artist Zoe Baldwin? Titles are up for grabs, including the position of creative design director at Ravens Cosmetics.

Zoe is one of those women who's planned out her life at an early age. She expects to end up seated at the corporate table at Ravens Cosmetics—not in the CEO's bed. But there's something to be said about the best-laid plans.

I must confess that I am one of those people who cannot leave the house without mascara. I wouldn't quite call it a dependency—more like a security blanket. And since I cannot seem to apply a wing tip or false lashes like a pro, I get to pay homage to the professionals in *The Beauty and the CEO*.

Carolyn

THE
Beauty
AND THE
CEO

Carolyn Hector

HARLEQUIN® KIMANI™ ROMANCE

Recycling programs
for this product may
not exist in your area.

ISBN-13: 978-0-373-86503-1

The Beauty and the CEO

Copyright © 2017 by Carolyn Hall

Printed in U.S.A.

HARLEQUIN®
www.Harlequin.com

Having your story read out loud as a teen by your brother in Julia Child's voice might scare some folks from ever sharing their work. But **Carolyn Hector** rose above her fear. She currently resides in Tallahassee, Florida, where there is never a dull moment. School functions, politics, football, Southern charm and sizzling heat help fuel her knack for putting a romantic spin on everything she comes across. Find out what she's up to on Twitter: @Carolyn32303.

Books by Carolyn Hector

Harlequin Kimani Romance

The Magic of Mistletoe
The Bachelor and the Beauty Queen
His Southern Sweetheart
The Beauty and the CEO

Visit the Author Profile page
at Harlequin.com for more titles.

I would like to dedicate this book to my ambitious daughter and nieces, Haley, Kayla and Ashleigh. I live vicariously through these talented young ladies.

Acknowledgments

I would like to acknowledge the Galaxy living in my house. Without their cooperation, I wouldn't get any writing done!

Chapter 1

Morning rays of sunlight created a halo effect around the godlike body of a six-foot-four man strolling through the parting glass doors of Kelly Towers. A collective gasp of soft feminine sighs rose over the swishing sound of the automatic doors closing. With the sun behind him, the man strolled down the red carpet toward the elevator right where makeup artist Zoe Baldwin stood.

Dear Lord, Zoe began her silent prayer, *if ever there were a time to get stuck in the elevator, please let it be now and with him.*

The denim jeans he wore clung to his powerful thighs. A thin, white, long-sleeved shirt hugged the sculpted muscles of his arms and abdomen. As he came closer, everyone in the lobby turned their heads in his direction. Thick, dark brows framed his eyes.

A prominent chin jutted out from the sharp angles of his long, masculine face. Zoe cocked her head to the left and reached up to touch the signature hoop earrings she was known to wear. Instead of the cool gold circle, Zoe's fingertip brushed against heirloom pearls handed down from her grandmother. The jewels had a reputation for good luck. Perhaps with this fine-as-hell gentleman coming closer, the hand-me-down stories were true.

Though he didn't carry a portfolio, Zoe pegged her soon-to-be elevator companion as a male model. The fifty-three-story Kelly Towers was home to several of Miami's elite businesses. The local news station was housed on ten floors, while Ravens Cosmetics, Zoe's final destination, was housed on the fortieth through the forty-ninth. Modeling and a few talent agencies were sprinkled throughout the other floors. Zoe guessed he'd get off on one of those floors. For her, the only place she needed to be was at Ravens Cosmetics—the home of the oldest and most successful cosmetic line for people of color in the United States and now globally. And if today went as planned at her interview, she could call Ravens Cosmetics home as well.

In an attempt to flirt, Zoe licked her lips, tasting the hint of honey in the concoction she used for lip balm. The response she received from the gorgeous man was a lopsided, boy-next-door smile mixed with a hint of danger. The sensual curve of his full lips begged to challenge the question every makeup-wearing woman pondered: Was he worth smearing her lipstick for? His lips parted into a dashing smile and crinkles appeared at the corners of his eyes. An older model? Twenty-five? Twenty-eight? She'd heard RC was going in a new direction. It was about time they added someone more age appropriate to their ads for men. The men in the ads for shaving, lotions and other male grooming products were handsome but also extremely young— as in barely-legal-young. Under thirty as a male was far from old, but in the modeling world he might be ready to retire.

"Hello," he said.

His deep baritone touched her soul. A powerful shiver trickled down her spine while her knees weakened. "Hi," she replied.

With the limited skills she had in the flirting department, Zoe batted her lashes and damn it if her cell phone didn't ring. The old-school Prince song indicated the hotline for one of her closest friends. It was almost a bat signal, and when that song rang, Zoe picked up the phone and answered. "Hey, what's up?"

Lexi Pendergrass Reyes's cheerful voice came over the line loud and clear. "I wanted to wish you luck before your interview."

"You're so sweet," Zoe said as she offered an apologetic smile to the handsome man. Zoe stepped backward and did a little spin in an attempt to give the stranger a better view of her angles in her black pencil skirt and red silk Rochas blouse decorated with oversize magnolias. She'd received the blouse at a *Vogue* photo shoot last year, another lucky memento of her work. "Can I call you right back?"

"Of course," Lexi said, "but don't forget. On top of wishing you the luck you don't need, I do have a huge favor to ask of you."

The flashing triangle light above the elevator doors

indicated it was coming in a few seconds. "The answer is yes. I don't even have to know what it is."

"You say that now. Bye, girl."

Zoe swiped the icon on her cell to hang up the call. She took a deep breath, ready to speak to her male model again. As a makeup artist, she noticed he needed no cover-up. She'd known some models and actors who'd paid to have cheekbones as sculpted as his.

"So," he began, leaning against the marble wall near the up and down arrow-shaped buttons of the elevator.

"So," Zoe repeated.

She was prepared to have some form of meaningful conversation in the span of the few seconds provided before the elevator arrived, but that was interrupted when the doors on the first floor, leading to the building's cafeteria, opened up. It was not unusual in a place like this to run into some of the local celebrities. A gaggle of girls screamed at the sight of Zoe. Zoe and her magic beauty box kits were the reason certain faces graced the covers of top beauty magazines. She'd decorated the faces of movie stars, governors and their spouses, singers and television reality stars. Torn between not having seen these ladies in quite some time and getting to the meat of this conversation with the hot guy, Zoe offered another apologetic smile. The man stepped forward and extracted a business card from his back pocket to give to her, then winked before turning to take the door into the stairwell.

"Hey, guys," said Zoe, slipping the card into the front of her purse. "What's going on today?"

The half-dozen girls began to complain all at once about having to come in this morning for a music video which was being filmed in the cafeteria. Something about their makeup not being right and begging Zoe to ace the interview.

"Girl, that outfit is giving me life! There really should be no reason for you to interview," said Clarita Benson. She was a six-foot-three model in flats.

The next tallest was six-two, a former volleyball star turned model. Her blond hair stuck out at the ends like straw. "I heard Marcus Ravens say you were the best person for the job."

"I guess we'll see in a little bit." Zoe shrugged her shoulders and craned her neck. Thankfully, the elevator doors opened with a loud ding. "Listen, ladies, I've got to head off and ace this interview."

The doors closed as the girls chorused, "Good luck!" Zoe leaned against the back of the compartment. She smiled at her reflection, knowing she'd dressed the part.

In truth, Zoe knew she was the right person for the position as the Creative Design Director at Ravens Cosmetics. She had a BS in biochemistry and an MS in cosmetic chemistry, both from Fairleigh Dickinson University, held a license as a beautician and was the number one most-requested makeup artist at Fashion Week in New York, London, Milan and Paris. Her work with artists at Coachella over the last five years had gotten her noticed for the CDD position at several cosmetic companies.

Zoe only wanted to set roots down in the Miami office of Ravens Cosmetics. Call it a predestined destination. Her great-grandmother Sadie, affectionately known as GiGi, ran one of the largest cosmetology schools in the Southeast. As a teen growing up in Trinidad, Gigi loved getting ready for the masquerade, also known as "Mas," at Carnival. For a touch of home, she named her new school after the beloved event. Before leaving Mas Beauty School, all the students wanted to be an employee at Ravens Cosmetics, one of the oldest and most successful cosmetics companies founded by an African American woman for people of color. It would be a sign of success to join their company. Tears of pride and joy threatened to escape the corners of her eyes as she realized how close she was to following in her grandmother's footsteps.

Just last week at the after-party of a successful swimsuit fashion show, RC's president, Marcus Ravens, had told Zoe the job was practically hers. The models on both of his arms swore Zoe was the best. And modestly Zoe had agreed.

Traveling in fashion circles, Zoe had met Marcus's other board members, a group made up of siblings and cousins from the large family. Each of the directors represented shareholders, the elders of Ravens Cosmetics.

It had been hard to gauge how some of the Ravens women felt about her. In the world of fashion and cosmetics, everyone was either an enemy or an ally. For a very brief moment in Zoe's life she'd modeled. Her knowledge of the industry, inside and out, put her in a threatening position. Plenty of times she'd overstepped the bounds as a makeup artist, questioning the chemicals the other cosmetologists wanted to put on someone's face. She almost became difficult to work with. With her degree in cosmetic chemistry she could easily start her own line. But Zoe wanted stability in her life. Her parents married young before they had a chance to live out their dreams, before settling down. Seeing her parents struggle to stay together while reaching their own goals put a damper on Zoe's outlook on relationships. Things were changing now. She was established and not to mention older than her parents had been when they married. Thirty was rapidly knocking on her door and a faint biological clock was ticking in the back of her mind.

Having reaffirmed her worth, Zoe took a deep breath. When the elevator dinged to announce her presence on the fortieth floor, the doors parted and opened up to a quieter situation than on the first floor. A half-circle African blackwood desk drew Zoe's attention immediately, along with a receptionist who had curly blond hair pulled up in a frizzy ponytail at the top of her head. A headset rested somewhere in the hair, Zoe guessed, because the girl held her finger up in Zoe's direction but finished the conversation on the other end of the line before disconnecting the call.

"Miss Baldwin?" The young girl, whose foundation was poorly blended from her face to neck, rolled her eyes at the sight of Zoe. *Clearly not a fan.*

Zoe smiled and nodded. "Yes, that's me."

"Okay, so, you and the others are in the waiting room over there."

The others? Using the eraser end of a pencil, the receptionist pointed toward a glass room adjacent to her desk. A minute ago Zoe had been giving herself a pep talk. She was sure the job was hers and she knew she'd earned it. But there were others? She stood at the glass door to the conference room where just over a half-dozen women and men sat waiting at a large oval table made of the same wood as the reception desk. In an instant, Zoe recognized everyone at the table, including Titus, her nemesis.

To make it to this level of her profession, Zoe had come across several—as the young model clients had called them—haters, and Titus was not her number one fan. The one-name wonder scowled through the glass at Zoe, his long, tacky feather lashes clumping together, causing him to have to pry them apart with his loud pink fingernails. Zoe refrained herself from rolling her eyes by sighing instead. The man claimed to be the best yet can't figure out which adhesive glue for lashes worked best. At the AJ Crimson event last year, Zoe'd almost had to tell him about himself when she found her artist's kit at his station. He claimed the kit was accidentally placed there but Zoe knew better. He tried to steal it. A makeup artist's beauty kit was as important to them as a doctor's stethoscope, a police officer's badge or even a mechanic's tools. Zoe admired AJ Crimson for becoming a leader in the beauty world, bringing his popular brand of cosmetics to pop culture through hip-hop music and current top television shows. How badly did she want the Creative Design Director position? Zoe took a step backward.

"You're not leaving, are you, Zoe?"

Zoe turned around at the sound of Marcus Ravens's voice. An automatic smile spread across her face at the sight of him. Marcus was a handsome man, tall, dark and charming. Zoe returned his friendly smile. All the models who did work for RC had gushed about him. "Hello, Marcus."

"Are you going in?" Marcus nodded his head at the door. The others inside craned their necks.

"I think there's been a misunderstanding," said Zoe.

Marcus retreated a step and glanced in both directions down the hall. He stepped closer to Zoe and touched her elbow. "There is, or was," he said and shook his head. "There has been a slight change of plans. You see, my brother is here."

Zoe slowly shook her head to the left and then the right. "Okay? I spoke with Donovan last week. He assured me the job is mine. All I'd have to do is meet with the board."

"It is yours," Marcus exclaimed. "You know you're the best person for the job."

"It seems someone thinks several people are the perfect person for the job." Zoe inclined her head toward the room of other makeup artists.

"That's what I'm trying to explain." There was a panic in Marcus's deep voice. He pressed one hand on Zoe's shoulders as a vein pulsed at his temples, which he tried to cover up by scratching the back of his neck with his other hand. "My brother—my other brother, Will—is responsible."

"Will?" Zoe repeated. "I thought I knew everyone in your family."

Back in middle school, Zoe had done one of her best biography reports on the Ravens family. She'd once known their family tree like the back of her hand. The Ravens started at the turn of the century selling beauty products to the wives of the men working on the railroad. It was Marcus's grandparents, Joe and Naomi Ravens, who'd slapped a label on their business and marketed it nationally. Zoe learned all about the following generations of Ravens through the Roaring Twenties and the forties to the present. The younger generations were all connected via social media. All of the family members worked for Ravens, right?

On numerous occasions Zoe had crossed paths with the Ravens family, either in the Miami Design District or at Miami's Fashion Week.

"He's our youngest brother, and my cousins nominated him to be the CEO of RC."

"Okay?" Zoe said slowly, still not following what that had to do with her and this interview.

"Will believes he should look at everyone interested in being the CDD."

Zoe's heart ached with a surge. "I'm not understanding, Marcus. You're the president."

"The CEO has a little more pull than the president," Marcus explained. "And right now, he's our last chance at keeping RC running."

The rumors were true. Someone wanted to shut down Ravens Cosmetics. Zoe's heart ached as if she'd been wronged. How could anyone think about dissolving this company? Five minutes ago she'd pumped herself up about wanting to board the RC ship. Now it felt like the ship was sailing away while she stood on the pier watching it depart. She asked herself again, how badly did she want to be the Creative Design Director?

"This is then a waste of my time, Marcus. I am too qualified to have to go through a screening process." Zoe turned to leave. Through the glass, Zoe thought she saw Titus mouthing something to her. She was not in the mood for a fight. "Either you like my work or you don't."

With his hands still on her shoulders, Marcus clamped down firmly. He turned her to face him so her back was to the receptionist area. "I do, my brothers and sisters do, and Will is going to feel the same way."

"You guys brought in Titus." A tic began to flutter underneath her right eye. The other makeup artist was good, of course he was. But he'd copied her trademark '80s style. This was too much stress for her. Zoe sighed impatiently. Great-Grandma Sadie would have a fit if she knew Zoe got this far only to abandon her own resolve. "I just can't deal with this, Marcus."

"Will you at least listen to me first? I'll get Donovan on the phone."

"I'm right here." Donovan's familiar voice filled the hallway.

Not wanting any pity, Zoe didn't dare turn around. Like his brother, Donovan had an extremely charismatic smile. Ever the charmer, he always knew how to bring out a natural blush on any model Zoe had worked on. If she glanced at Donovan, Zoe knew she'd swoon, and right now she was too pissed off to be cheered up. She kept her angry focus on the Windsor knot of Marcus's tie.

"Tell her everything is still going on as planned," Marcus said over her head to his brother.

"The interviewing process?" Donovan asked, and Marcus nodded. "It's just a process."

"Someone too good for an interview?" Another deep voice asked.

While the voice may have been sexy, the tone was not. Zoe spun on her heels, prepared to give this person a piece of her mind when she stopped and gaped. Instead of the fitted shirt and jeans she'd seen him in earlier at the elevator, he now wore a tailored, classically cut two-thousand-dollar navy blue suit with a blue-and-yellow paisley tie. Suits made Zoe's knees weak the same way lingerie did men's.

"You?" The man brushed roughly against Donovan's shoulders without apologizing.

"You?" Zoe repeated. "I don't understand." Zoe wondered how she hadn't recognized the similarities.

"Will, this is Zoe Baldwin, the woman we've been talking about." Donovan clamped his hands on his brother's back. "Zoe, this is our baby brother, Will."

"You're a makeup artist?"

"She's the *B* in Beauty Business," Donovan interjected.

So, the man from the elevator wasn't a struggling model? Judging from the expensive suit he wore, he was far from struggling. Zoe shrugged her shoulders indifferently. "Artist, genius, whatever you want to call me is fine."

"How about we keep it simple and call you interviewee number six?" Will asked.

Gone was the charming smile from downstairs. Zoe's hand brushed against the front pocket where she shoved his business card. She extracted it and fingered the raised letters, assuming it gave the three initials of his position. CEO. Jesus Christ, this man with a dry sense of humor held her fate in his hands. Somewhere in the back of her mind Zoe heard the proverbial ship sound its horn and sail off into the ocean.

At six in the evening, Will Ravens sat back in his newly ordered chair and tried to get the feel of it and the new position. He was in over his head. As a former professional soccer player for the Texas Raiders, the only thing he knew about women was what he was attracted to. Not being raised in the family business, Will did not possess the same keen cosmetic eye as his siblings. He knew what he'd liked and what he'd seen in the portfolios from the interviews this afternoon. There was nothing to catch his eye—but that wasn't necessarily true. The woman's face from earlier this afternoon entered his mind. He thumbed through the portfolios of the potential CDDs. A silver paper clip fastened to the manila folder secured a photo of Zoe Baldwin's heart-shaped face to the outside.

How was she the woman behind the makeup and not on the runway? Her flawless sienna-and-gold skin was radiant. Her chestnut-brown hair, secured today at the back of her neck, did not do her justice as the photograph before him did. In it, her mane hung over her shoulders and she smiled for the camera with one raised brow and a playful smile across her face.

"So, what did you think of Zoe Baldwin?"

Will dropped the portfolio at the unexpected interruption and cursed under his breath. "Jesus, Donovan, don't you knock?"

"We're family."

"All the more reason to knock," Will joked. The last round of complaints from their cousins were due to Donovan's dating the models. He went through at least one on a weekly basis. They threw themselves at him. The one thing a lot of models wanted more than a modeling contract for a spread in an RC ad was to land one of the Ravens men. Having his brothers in charge of anything dealing with models was as productive as letting a fox guard a henhouse. Fortunately, Will, the youngest of the men, had more common sense.

Less than ten years ago, the new generation of Ravens had been placed on the board. Everyone owned an equal share of Ravens Cosmetics. Half of Will's cousins wanted to dismantle the company. They were tired of the meetings and responsibilities. Will knew his great-grandparents were rolling in their graves at the idea. For the cousins, even the limited time they had to spend in the office was still too much. Will and his siblings, along with a handful of cousins, wanted to keep the legacy alive. The problem was, they were a band of eight against a band of another eight.

Donovan nodded his head. "Alright, you got me there." He stepped inside Will's office and made himself comfortable in one of the matching leather seats in front of Will's desk. "So, I'll ask you again, what did you think of Zoe?"

"Which one was she?" Will needed to play dumb. When the position opened up, Will was skeptical when Donovan suggested Zoe Baldwin. Given Donovan's track record, Will didn't want to risk any form of lawsuit. Given the chemistry Will felt when he spotted Zoe at the elevator, Will did not want to admit his attraction to a potential employee.

Gossip spread like wildfires in office settings. Kelly Towers, and all the businesses housed on the floors, was not immune to the tabloids. Home to the local news station, celebrity appearances and eager folks trying to catch a break in the media world, this building was often the target of tabloid spies. Will prided himself on his discretion. He took dating a person seriously. In a building filled with scantily clad women and men representing everything Ravens Cosmetics had to offer, spotting the demure woman at the elevator had been the highlight of his life for the last few weeks. Will's days of going through women were over. He was tired of women impressed by and after his money. Will never realized how much he appreciated the classic beauty of a woman until he'd seen her. She'd worn a simple skirt, a somewhat loud red blouse and pearls at her ears, as well as around her slender neck. When was the last time a woman wore pearls around her neck as a part of an outfit—not several strands of pearls as an outfit?

Will summed up Zoe Baldwin in one word: beautiful. There had been an instant connection between them when he walked into the hallway downstairs. It had been the first time he'd actually passed out one of the business cards he was given when he took on his role of CEO. If his brothers and sisters knew Will had almost asked her out today, they'd never leave him alone about it. His cousins would never trust his decisions if he acted like Donovan or Marcus.

"Y'all talking about the interviews today?" Marcus asked, poking his head in the door.

"Yes," Donovan said, leaning back in his chair to look at their oldest brother. "And Will is trying to act like he doesn't know which one Zoe was."

Marcus chuckled and entered the room. He took the seat next to Donovan and propped his elbows on Will's desk. "The one you drooled so much over, we needed to get the cleaning crew to mop up the saliva? The one who caused the hallway to become so sexually charged when she and Will laid eyes on each other?"

It was going to take some time for Will to get used to being around his family like this. Luckily his sisters, Dana and Eva, were out of town at a convention. They would already have started planning his wedding. Will needed to get used to the idea of carrying on his grandparents' corporate legacy before he thought about adding to it.

"You ought to go into creative writing," Will said with a dry yawn.

"I've got my hands full being president." Marcus glanced down at his fingers.

As Marcus inspected his cuticles, Donovan and Will dramatically bowed down at the president, a teasing move they did every time Marcus felt the need to inform them of his title. No one *wanted* to be the president. The president was the face of the company with not as much power as people believed. But if anyone needed to be the face, it was Marcus. He was what Will considered pretty, with soft brown hair and deeply tanned skin, helped out a bit by the Miami sun.

Thanks to a car accident a few years ago, Donovan never wanted to be in the public eye. He wanted to hide the long scar down his cheek from the cameras. No matter the differences Will saw between himself and his brothers, everywhere they went, people always knew they were siblings.

"You guys are jerks, you know that?" asked Marcus with a tight smile.

"You guys nominated me, a guy with no credibility in the business other than my last name, to be the CEO while I was recuperating," Will said drily. "So sue me if I don't feel sorry for you."

"By 'recuperating—'" Donovan raised his hands for air quotes "—you mean you were at your sci-fi convention?"

Will pressed his hands on top of the portfolios. "I believe you were right there next to me in a Flash mask."

Marcus's head snapped toward Donovan. "You said you were in New York."

"I was, right after Comic-Con."

Before his brothers went off on a tangent, Will cleared his throat. "Let's talk about the interviews today. I'd like to be on a united front before we meet back with the cousins."

His grandparents carried on a long family tradition of creating products for the community. They'd raised their six kids in a modest four-bedroom home in Overtown, a predominately African American neighborhood in Miami. His great-great-grandmother had sold hair-care products to the women whose husbands worked on the railroads. Skin-care and hair-care products had helped mold the Ravens into a millionaire family back in the day. Will wanted to make sure Ravens Cosmetics made it to one hundred years in business.

Will concentrated on his brothers in front of him. "Who did y'all like?"

"Zoe," Donovan and Marcus chorused.

Will liked Zoe, but he wasn't sure it was for the same reasons as his brothers. It wasn't like Will to arrive at RC late, as he had that morning. His cousins Katie and Dixon had conveniently forgotten to remind him of the time change for the interviews. And to make matters worse, he'd worked out with Dixon this morning. No wonder Dixon had hopped off the treadmill a few miles sooner than normal. Will should have known better. These cousins were ready to dissolve Ravens Cosmetics. He frowned. Will refused to let that happen on his watch.

"I'm not sure she's what I had in mind for such a position."

"And what did you have in mind?"

Flipping open the portfolio with Zoe's face on it, Will thumbed through the photographs of all the women and men she'd worked on. "This work is too busy for me. We're here to support the everyday woman, and she paints a face like they're eighties rock stars."

"Paints a face?" Marcus snickered as if he'd said something erroneous. "What's wrong with that?"

"I want to go in a different direction. I want something more classic." Will sat back in his seat and poised his fingers like a steeple. "Like a 1940s look."

"You want to start a new retro look?" asked Donovan.

"See, that's what is wrong with you two." Will shrugged his shoulders and continued without waiting for an answer. "What's wrong with it? Everyone else is looking for these loud colors and makeup so heavy the girls resemble raccoons. I'm trying to save the company with something new this generation hasn't experienced."

"And you think you can bring classic back? Women evolved from that style, as well. Zoe is hot right now."

Will shrugged again. Yes, Zoe was hot now and if she worked here, she'd also be un-dateable. "Hey, you guys put me in this position. I can take it, but you are going to have to trust me on this. Tell me the truth, do you really want to bring your lady to Sunday dinner looking like this?" Will held up one of the jobs Zoe had done and shook his head. At the elevator she'd given off a classic vibe, but her body of work on paper did not interest him. "No, I want to take things in a new direction. Trust me."

Chapter 2

By the time Zoe turned the lock on her door at the Cozier Condos off Biscayne Boulevard, she was tired and heartbroken. *Humiliated* was a better description of her day. Never before had she expected to go through the stressful interview process to prove her worth. Well, maybe not never. Once she'd had to interview for the job as a scoop girl at The Scoop's Ice Cream Parlor back in Southwood, Georgia, when Zoe's love for makeup had exceeded her allowance. She had to prove to the owners she loved ice cream and all of the flavors they had to offer. Hopefully Zoe's most stressful interviews would be her first and her last.

The set of house keys jingled with a clink into the clear bowl on top of the credenza. The weight of the keys shifted the bowl into yesterday's mail, nudging the silver box with gold writing on top. The latest Ravens Cosmetic Artist Kit filled with fabulous foundation colors had arrived, along with the silver tubes of lipstick. Zoe broke out one bullet-shaped container and inspected the color—No Shade. Usually these beauty boxes excited her, but today's mood rippled with disappointment.

When in doubt, Zoe always called on a hometown friend for advice. On her phone, she pressed the icon she had for Lexi—a tiara—and waited for the beauty queen to answer. While Lexi had gone to a different school during the year, she came home to Southwood for the summers and she and her friends had taken Zoe under their wing.

Lexi answered on the second ring. "How did it go today?"

"It was nothing like I expected," Zoe drawled. She set the phone on the counter and swiped the speaker button for a hands-free conversation while she fiddled around in her condo's kitchen. "I had to wait in the conference room like a person trying to…" Zoe lost her words.

"Get a job?" Lexi provided.

Even though Lexi couldn't see, Zoe rolled her eyes. "Whatever. I have a job. Several of them. Did you forget the MET Awards are coming up next in August and Fashion Week after that?"

Celebrities were already requesting Zoe's help for the big event for Multi-Ethnic Television. She had high-profile weddings in the Midwest on the schedule as well, and a few more job interviews up north. Travel was her middle name. At least the MET event was going to be held in Orlando this year.

"But you want just the one. You wanted to be in

a permanent spot." Lexi reminded her. "Or, at least, that's what you told me the last time we spoke. I bet your suitcase isn't even unpacked from your stint in Hollywood."

Since her overnight bag was still by her laundry-room door, Zoe decided not to confirm Lexi's state-ment. Instead, she hummed a little ditty for a moment while her eyes searched the kitchen counter for some-thing to eat. Finding the bag of roti from Trudy's, the local West Indian market and restaurant around the corner, Zoe grabbed a piece of the bread made from stone-ground flour and went to the refrigerator for the questionable leftover curry from last week. While the food heated up, Zoe grabbed the phone, took it off the stand and headed off toward her bedroom. Her apart-ment had only two bedrooms, a small living room and a dinette and kitchen, but it was home—subleased, but still home.

"I can still call in some favors with RC," said Lexi.

It seemed there wasn't a person in the fashion world Lexi did not know. Her store, Grits and Glam Gowns, was renowned. As women flocked there for dresses, whether for proms, pageants or weddings, a mention of her product meant everything in the world to a com-pany. Lexi had a lot of power.

"No." Zoe shook her head. "I want to earn this job without any favors. The president told me I'm golden. But this round of interviews is thanks to their new CEO."

"So, who is the CEO of RC now?" Lexi asked. "Donovan?"

"No," Zoe groaned. "His name is Will Ravens."

"Wait, the soccer player?"

"No." Zoe hummed a noise again, kicking out of her heels and footing them into the closet. "He's the CEO. Donovan and Marcus introduced him to us."

"Is he hot, like his brothers?" asked Lexi.

"Lexi!" Zoe gasped, wanting more than anything to elaborate on exactly how hot Will Ravens was. "You're married with a baby on the way."

"I'm married, not blind," Lexi reminded her. "If it's who I think it is, William Ravens played soccer and was hurt during a game. I want to say a broken leg."

Slipping out of her skirt, Zoe padded barefoot into the bathroom. "Since when did you become the sports fan?"

"You can thank my beautiful husband for that." Lexi giggled on the other end of the line. Zoe thought it was a nice laugh. She wanted something like that one day. A man who made her blush just by thinking of him. "I'm pretty sure he paused the match to show me the horrific leg break," Lexi went on.

The corners of Zoe's lips turned down. "Ouch. Well, this Will Ravens did not show signs of any leg injury."

As a matter of fact, Zoe thought wantonly, she thought his strut was rather sexy. At least, she had when she thought he was simply a model. As a makeup artist, Zoe was constantly around handsome men. None of them ever had her wanting to jump in a cold shower. How was it going to work out when she got the job at RC? Zoe shrugged and pushed the thought out of her mind.

"Lexi, what was it you were going to ask me earlier?"

"Oh, that. I need you to come home for an event next week," said Lexi. "I'm hosting the Miss South-wood Glitz Pageant and I need a nonbiased makeup artist. Please say you'll come. I've booked up Magnolia Palace from Monday to next Sunday. All the judges and working staff will start coming in Tuesday. I want everyone to get to know each other so they can trust their opinions when it comes time to voting and making this the best pageant ever."

The mere mention of the old hotel, Magnolia Palace, evoked a memory of Zoe's youth. She closed her eyes and heard the sound of her bare feet pounding down the wooden planks as she raced to jump off the bridge. Her parents met on that same bridge. Her mother had been a model and her father out fishing. He'd certainly snagged the biggest catch of his life that day. "Now, how am I going to say no to an offer like that?"

"You're not," Lexi laughed.

"Since I won't be starting my CDD position any time soon, I'll be there. Text me the details."

Zoe swiped her phone to the off screen and stood in the center of her bedroom, contemplating what to do next. She was hungry, but the recent talk of Will Ravens began to make her sweat—again. A shower would do her some good, then she'd eat the curry.

Fifteen minutes after her ice-cold shower, Zoe padded barefoot back into her kitchen and reheated her food. She'd slipped her cell phone into the front pocket of her fluffy pink bathrobe and felt it vibrate on her thigh as she sat at the counter.

You were great today. A decision will be made in a few weeks.

Zoe reread Marcus's text message two more times. How was she supposed to go to bed tonight knowing she hadn't secured the position of Creative Design Director? Her life was being held up by a man she knew nothing about. Where had he gone to school? Had he been a business major or something in the field of cosmetic chemistry? What had Lexi said? He'd played sports before deciding to join the family business? A feeling of dread sunk to the pit of her stomach at the thought of her life being upheld by an athlete. At least she knew that by the weekend she'd be back home in Southwood and away from the drama for a while.

Will didn't look up from the rest of the portfolios after his brothers left to pick up dinner. In soccer he'd put in his time on the field and in the locker room. He spent more time on the field finessing his skills than in the club, like some of his teammates. Will knew the odds were against him. He had no training and no experience other than on the soccer field. Since coming to RC, Will couldn't remember getting home before the sun set. Trudy's, the West Indian market and restaurant down the block, saw more of him than his own kitchen.

The grandfather clock in the corner of the office chimed eight. A smile tugged at his mouth. When they were kids, he and his brothers used to play hide-and-seek on this floor of the building. Will's favorite place was in here, where Grandpa Joe shared the office space with his wife. With a chuckle, Will realized why they'd shared an office. If Grandma was going to stay late at work, so was Grandpa. It must have been nice to have someone who stayed with you if you couldn't get home on time.

Now that he wasn't traveling full time or training, Will wondered if any of that would happen to him.

Would he have someone to share office space with, or who would sit back with a knowing smile as his children played in here? Grandma Naomi was going on ninety. So far, her six children had blessed her with over a dozen grandchildren.

The stack of portfolios in front of him moved and the top folder shifted. A knock at his door sounded and brought Will out of his daze.

Through the glass door he spotted his identical twin cousins, Joyce and Naomi. Each was beautiful enough to be the face of RC. They were easily six feet tall, with high cheekbones and perfectly arched brows that they loved to raise at Will during their meetings whenever he asked a question about their marketing department. Will considered them allies in this war to dismantle RC. He waved them in.

Joyce, the older by seven minutes, sat down first in one of the chairs in front of his desk. Naomi, however, crossed the room to admire the photographs Will refused to throw away.

"What's going on, ladies?"

"We have a great suggestion for you," said Joyce.

Will sat back in his seat and silently prayed for Marcus and Donovan to return with dinner. Whatever the girls wanted from him, they'd decided to team up.

The reason they worked so well together was they were complete opposites. Joyce was more business oriented. Naomi was more of the partying type, ironic since she was their grandmother's namesake. Joyce had more of the ninety-year-old woman's personality, business first.

"Uh-oh, do I need reinforcements?" Will teased and pretended to pick up the black office phone on the corner of his desk. "Marcus and Donovan should be back any minute now."

"What we are suggesting," said Naomi from her corner of the room, "your brothers will wholeheartedly agree to, since it will be good for business."

The deep breath he took brought in her coconut scent, a perfume he recognized from Ravens Cosmetics. "Alright."

"With you coming on as the new CEO—"

"Coming on?" Will repeated, flabbergasted. "Why does everyone say that as if I had a choice? I believe the two of you were the first ones to second the nomination, knowing good and well I'm out of my league."

Naomi rolled her eyes. "I would have nominated you first, but Charles beat me to it."

"Anyway," Naomi huffed. "If you are serious about turning things around, we think it would be a great idea for you to fly up to Southwood, Georgia, as our representative."

"Where?" Will began flipping through the paperwork on his desk. His frat brother, Dominic Crowne, recently moved his luxury car business to a town with that name.

"Exactly," said Joyce. She leaned forward, resting her elbows on the desk. "I need you to be someplace out of your element. I want you to be a judge at this beauty pageant a business associate of RC's is having."

The only thing Will could think of was some guy in a tuxedo holding a long-stemmed microphone and singing to a crowned woman. "No."

"Will," Joyce and Naomi wailed.

"What do I know about beauty pageants?"

"You're a guy, right?" Naomi asked, and answered

without waiting for a response. "You just vote on who the prettiest is."

Zoe Baldwin's smiling face at the elevator popped into his mind. He'd already met the prettiest woman. "I don't want to do it. Get Marcus or Donovan."

"Seriously?" Naomi asked drily. "There's a reason we've learned to knock on the office doors of your brothers. C'mon, Will. It's important you make a name for yourself."

"Look, Will," Joyce snapped, "Ravens Cosmetics is the sponsor at this pageant every year. If you don't do it, it will be someone like Charles or Brandon or even Dixon. You and I both know that isn't what we need right now, especially with our other choices being your horndog brothers."

"Seriously? Me?"

Joyce shrugged her shoulders. "Over the years, Lexi Reyes has been a great asset for Ravens Cosmetics." She gave a brief history about their former beauty queen and her golden touch, and how the company had been sponsoring her pageants for years. This was the first Will had ever heard of it.

"And so, if you help Lexi out, it will give RC a platform to change the way some consumers see us—we're not simply retro but classic, like you've suggested. Our brand will be the only one used for the pageant. Our gift bags of mascara, eye shadows and lotions will go to all the attendees. Do you know how many Southern women attend pageants? Our research shows most women below the Mason-Dixon Line aren't interested in the avant-garde. We can tap into this community and save RC. And that's what you claimed you wanted to do. Or was that a lie?"

"Hell, no." Will slammed his hand on the top of the portfolios. "I don't care what our cousins think. RC is not dead." Will's gut twisted with doubt. The twins made a great point. What he lacked in experience, he made up for in determination. RC was not dead and had another hundred years left. He didn't want to risk ignoring a potential market. But a beauty pageant? He hated himself for being suckered in. "Okay, fine, send me the information. What night do I have to be there?"

"Well, here's the thing," Naomi started. "In order for you to be there and be able to mesh with the other judges, you need to be there for maybe a week."

"What?" Will exclaimed.

Joyce held her hands up to calm him down. "It won't be that bad."

"I just started here last month. I don't have a week to give." He calculated the forty-plus hours a week he'd already been putting in and knew that time was still not enough. His cousins would be hovering like vultures if he left his throne for more than a few days.

"Think about how committed the family will see you are if you take the time to represent our products."

She had to go there. Will's weakness. His family's legacy was his kryptonite. Sales were down. People were losing interest in Ravens Cosmetics. They wanted something fresh and new. Well, if anyone could go to this Southwood and turn things around, it was him. "When do I leave?"

Armed with a suitcase filled with cosmetics, Zoe checked her bags at the counter at Miami International Airport on Tuesday morning and got herself cleared through security. If she was lucky, her plane would be there, allowing her to board.

This wasn't her first trip on a plane. She knew it was best to take a change of clothes in her carry-on. No matter how long or short the flight, Zoe always showered after traveling. For this two-hour flight, Zoe dressed in a pair of comfy boyfriend jeans, worn white canvas shoes and her favorite loose T-shirt, bedazzled in pink with Wear More Mascara across the chest. As she rounded the corner toward her terminal, she realized she had no such luck. And every seat in the waiting area was taken. Children pressed their faces against the windows, smudging the glass with their sticky hands as they watched the other planes taking off.

Zoe had no patience to deal with the man standing behind her she just caught checking out her rear end. The joker wasn't even embarrassed; he wiggled his brows at her and licked his lips. The only man on Earth, as far as Zoe was concerned, who was allowed to lick his lips at her was LL Cool J.

"Miss Baldwin?" Will Ravens closed the gap from the private area to where she stood. "I thought I recognized you."

For a moment, Zoe forgot how to speak. Will Ravens, the man she needed to hate right now, stood before her in a pair of jeans and a fitted green V-neck shirt, causing her to melt into a puddle as he smiled at her. Dark hairs were sprinkled across his sculpted jaw. A white sign in front of the blue terminal waiting room where he stood alone indicated the area was for passengers detoured from the hangar. Was the private area for other jets, full planes or those under construction? Zoe's mind raced with questions. Why was he here? Where was he going? How did she look? "Mr. Ravens?"

"Is everything okay?" he asked with a tilt of his head.

Blinking and then nodding, Zoe laughed lightly. "Oh, yes, sorry. I must have airport brain."

"That's a thing?" Will asked with a crooked grin.

"Yeah, you know, when you have fear of flying." Zoe inclined her head in the direction of the crowded terminal. "Not necessarily with the whole airplane thing, but who you're going to end up sitting with."

Will glanced in the direction she'd indicated and Zoe's eyes followed. Without any regard for the man currently standing next to her, another stranger blew a kiss at her. "Is it safe to assume you don't want to end up sitting next to him?"

An Elvis Presley snarl stretched Zoe's top lip as she shivered. "Exactly."

"You could end up sitting next to me," said Will.

Zoe gave her undivided attention back to the hunk before her. "Like *you* would fly commercial."

"I've flown commercial before." Will frowned. The corners of his lips turned upside down in the cutest way. "I wasn't born with a silver spoon in my mouth."

As she took a step backward, Zoe folded her arms across her chest and cocked one questioning brow. Everything about him screamed one percent.

Will pressed his hand against his heart and bowed his head. "For the record, I've been on the company plane just a few times."

"And today makes what? Your tenth time on your private plane?"

In response, Will nodded his dark head. "Every three commercial trips we get a bonus. We get to bring a guest with us. What do you say? Can I give you a lift?" The humorous tone matched the smirk on his face.

Uncrossing her arms, Zoe shook her head to the side. "What do I say to what?"

"A ride, you know, to wherever you're going."

It was as if he was asking her to share his cab with her or giving her a lift from the grocery store. So simple. So easy. *So tempting.* "You don't even know where I'm going."

At the most inconvenient time, a woman's voice came over the intercom. "All passengers heading for Atlanta, we will begin boarding in ten minutes."

"I'll take a wild guess and say you're headed to Atlanta."

The idea of squeezing into a seat next to either one of those two men, Will or the man who'd been behind her, did not sit well with Zoe. On the other hand, flying with Will might give her the chance to show off her work. "You can't be serious."

"But I am."

"I don't want to take you out of your way," Zoe said chewing on her bottom lip. So many images of having him her way entered her mind. "Where were you headed?"

"If I were to tell you, it wouldn't even matter. Just know that I am headed in the direction of Atlanta and I don't mind at all giving you a lift."

In truth, this deal had been sealed when Will broached the subject. But when one of the kids across

the hall screamed he was going to be sick and pro-
ceeded to do so, Zoe was sold.

"Well—" Zoe hesitated with another gnaw on her
bottom lip "—you wouldn't even have to take me all
the way to Atlanta. My friend was going to pick me
up and bring me down south."

Will stepped aside and waved his arm in the direction of the terminal. "Where exactly are you headed?"

Elated to not have to fly on the crowded plane, Zoe
stepped forward into the blue area. "A little town called
Southwood," she called over her shoulder. She walked
a few more paces before she realized Will was not behind her. She turned around and found him standing
in the same spot. "What's wrong?"

"Are you attending this Glitz-something pageant?"

A slow smile spread across Zoe's face. "What do
you know about it?"

"My cousins, Joyce and Naomi, talked me into
going. They said it would be good for business if I
represented the company as a judge."

"Smart move," Zoe said with a slight nod of the
head. Right now, hearing anything about the twins
soured her thoughts. A month or two ago, Marcus had
told her about the position at Ravens Cosmetics and got
her hopes up. Zoe was supposed to have been a sure
thing. Yet here she was, stuck at MIA, contemplating
hitching a ride with the man who lacked the ability to
see her talents. Zoe cleared her throat.

"I've got nothing but smart moves planned for the
company," Will said.

Zoe felt the corners of her eyes tighten with a smirk.
Her body leaned forward. She expected Will to add
something along the lines of "when you join the team."

All she received was a sneer. "What do you know about the beauty industry?" Zoe boldly asked.

"I know I'm not going to let my family's legacy fail," he retorted.

Without him having to say the words, Zoe knew Will was not impressed with her work. Seemed like this week was going to turn out perfect.

When Will flashed a smile, her knees went weak again. According to Lexi's itinerary, they were going to be sequestered for almost a week. Zoe would be making over all of the contestants. One full week to prove to Will she'd be the perfect person for the CDD job.

A man wearing a dark suit and aviator glasses appeared at the entranceway of the door leading toward the plane. In a ripple effect, the man Zoe assumed was the pilot nodded his head at Will, Will returned the head nod and, in turn, inclined his head to Zoe. "There's my guy," Will said. "There's someone more important in the hangar…"

"You mean more than you?" Zoe gasped sarcastically, her hand clutched to her heart.

"Cute," he said with a sigh. "So, what's it going to be, Miss Baldwin?"

"I'll go," Zoe said hesitantly, "but understand that I am going to have to owe you a ride."

The way Will raised his brows made her shiver with wanton promise. She pressed her lips together and shook her head. Flashes of her naked body curled up in a mixture of his arms and tangled sheets entered her mind. Heat began to boil underneath her shirt. "You know what I'm talking about."

"I certainly do," Will said.

The only thing Zoe could do was pray Will hadn't

felt the dampness on her lower back as he pressed his hand there to guide her across the windy airport strip toward the plane. Once they boarded, Zoe realized they were the only ones taking up space on the twenty-two pearl-leather seats. A flight attendant, dressed in a cute thigh-length lavender button-down dress with gold and pearl accessories—staple colors of Ravens Cosmetics packaging—greeted them as they boarded. She lifted her arm effortlessly to point in the direction of all the available seats.

Ahead of Will, Zoe glanced in the direction of the restrooms. Did the mile-high club count if they were the only ones on the plane? She jumped when Will touched the back of her shoulders. His thumb circled the nape of her neck.

"We have our pick," said Will, "but these are my favorites." His gentle touch against her skin guided her to a set of seats facing one another with a round coffee table between them. She imagined all the business deals made over that table.

"Thank you again, Mr. Ravens," Zoe replied with a curt nod of her head.

The perky flight attendant came over to take their order for drinks. Both of them asked for bottled water. When they were alone again, the captain began to take off. Out of the window, Zoe watched her plane still sitting on the runway. Will sat across from her. His long legs stretched out and their knees touched. Zoe sat straighter and crossed her legs together at the ankles.

"Having doubts?" Will's deep voice brought Zoe out of her zone. She blinked into focus and he explained further. "About coming on the plane with me?"

Zoe kept a straight face and led things in a professional direction. "I do appreciate this. I'm honored to have another chance to speak with you."

"Are you now?" Will asked with a raised brow.

"Of course," said Zoe, reaching for her phone from her purse. Her fingers slid across the screen to bring it to life. "This gives me more time to show you what you may not have seen in my portfolio."

"And give you an advantage over the other artists?"

A cold chill rushed down Zoe's spine and she offered a tight smile. She slid the phone back in her purse. "Have you ever been to Southwood before?"

"Can't say that I have," said Will, crossing one long leg over the other.

Zoe inhaled deeply at the way his thighs rippled beneath the denim. "Well, you're in for a treat. It's like taking a walk into history."

"Uh," Will started, "our history in the South?"

"Just wait and see."

"I take it you've been there?"

Nodding, Zoe grinned. "I spent my summers there and the last two years of high school."

"Your parents aren't together?"

No one ever asked about her parents. When working, she did most of the talking with her clients. Zoe usually eased models' fears of being in front of a particular photographer or clients' nervousness about the events Zoe was getting them ready for. To them, she was a machine. Will made her feel like a person. "They're together in a sense," she answered, and then nodded. "They never divorced, but they never truly lived together. My mother, Jamerica, is from Trinidad and she couldn't stand being away from the islands for too long. And, well, my dad preferred to be landlocked."

The corners of Will's mouth turned down. "Does he still live there now?"

"Worried about meeting my father?"

Will uncrossed his legs and leaned forward with his elbows on his knees. "I haven't done anything to you yet to be worried about."

A chill of excitement ran down Zoe's spine. What kinds of things would he do? Just the thought of his lips on her collarbone steamed her throughout her body. Even with her last official relationship, Zoe never day-dreamed about what his lips would do. Shaun Jackson had been sweet, hunky and driven, but never enough for Zoe to get distracted from her own goals. This was a perfect example of why she carried a change of clothes with her in her carry-on bag. Zoe cleared her throat and tried to stay focused on the prize. What she wanted was the Creative Design Director position. She was not going to sleep her way to the top. She'd never had to before, and she wasn't going to start now.

"Alright, I'll drop it for now," Will said, interrupting her thoughts. "Will you be staying at your father's?"

Zoe shook her head. "Dad is away this summer. But, even so, I won't be staying there."

An inquisitive brow rose on Will's face. "No?"

"I heard that everyone involved with the pageant is going to be at Magnolia Palace."

"Is it someplace special? My cousins gushed when they told me about it."

"I am biased," Zoe began, a smile touching her face at the vast memories. "My folks met there when my mother was on a photo shoot. He proposed there, as well."

A sad sigh struggled in the back of Zoe's throat. She wanted what her parents had, minus the not living together. A long-distance relationship worked for them, but not her. As much as work kept Zoe busy, she didn't have time to nurture a relationship. Soon Zoe was going to want someone she could wake up to every day. Work had always been important and the proverbial *someday* lurked around the corner. Once she got the position at Ravens Cosmetics, Zoe planned on settling down. There were a few potential men in Miami, but no one worth giving up her goals for. Zoe needed a man as driven as herself.

"Well, I can't wait to see this place," Will concluded with a dazzling grin.

"Me, either," Zoe beamed. "During high school, Magnolia Palace sort of crashed and burned. But recently it was bought and renovated. I'm excited to see the changes and I can't wait to walk along the pier."

For a moment, Zoe held her breath. Given her creative job as a makeup artist, she lived in a fast-paced world. People wanted fast-paced things. A walk along a pier on a lake was not fast-paced.

Will nodded his dark head. "Well then, I am excited to see it and take this walk, as well."

A spark went off in Zoe's heart and another heat wave of desire coursed through her veins. What she needed more than anything was a splash of cold water across her face. Maybe taking this flight had been a bad idea after all. With a combination of these close quarters, Will's sexy smiles and not having sex in six months, her senses were on high alert. Still determined to see Will as her future boss, Zoe rose from her seat and started to move around the coffee table. At the most inconvenient time, the small aircraft hit an air pocket, sending Zoe stumbling right into Will's lap.

Graciously he opened his arms and accommodated her on his lap until the turbulence ceased. One of his hands braced her back and the other secured her thighs against him. Another jolt sent Zoe's arms flailing and, rather than hit him in the face, she wrapped them around his shoulders, bringing them nose to nose. Zoe inhaled deeply. One millimeter closer and their lips would be touching.

"Ahem." The flight attendant cleared her throat from her end of the plane. Zoe scrambled out of Will's lap and headed off to the bathroom. "The captain sends his apologies and wanted to let you know we'll be landing shortly."

Zoe closed the door behind her and an overhead light turned on. A deep red tint stained her cheeks. What had she almost done? She wanted the job. But not this way. This really was going to be the longest week ever.

Chapter 3

Check-in at the Magnolia Palace started at noon. Thanks to the fact that there had been no more turbulence, Will and Zoe were able to land practically in the backyard of Southwood, Georgia, and arrive in town extra early. Dominic Crowne had moved his business, Crowne Motors Restoration, here because he wanted a quiet place in the country. Dominic restored classic cars and test-drove them on his private track; he imported foreign vehicles, as well. Dominic and Will had pledged together at Stanford. They were friends as freshmen, but brothers by graduation.

When Will had played in Germany with the Teufels, Dominic came to every match when he was in town. After Will returned to the States with the Texas Raiders, Dominic had come to his matches whenever he was close enough. In fact, Dominic was at the game when

Will had failed to qualify for the World Cup team. The limp was faint, the scar healed, but the painful disappointment of his lifelong dream being taken away from him would remain.

Will's thoughts turned to the passenger seated comfortably next to him in the shiny black 1963 Maserati 3500 Vignale Spyder, loaned to him by Dominic. Ever since Zoe had plopped down on his lap during the turbulence, Will couldn't get her out from under his skin. Even while teasing him, she dazzled him with her smile. It was too early to tell if the smile she offered was from the woman he met at the elevator or the woman who wanted the position.

"And you're telling me you don't come from a privileged background?" Zoe was saying, apparently oblivious to the way she made him feel. Her arms were folded across her chest, making her cleavage more noticeable in her V-neck T-shirt.

Will glanced over and felt the tension in his shoulders leave at the sight of her easy smile. "Hey, membership has its privileges."

Zoe's lashes fluttered against her high cheekbones. The sun spilled through the windshield and highlighted the gold tones of her dark skin. A pair of gold earrings highlighted her cheekbones. "I guess I can't complain too much. I might still be sitting on the plane in coach if it weren't for you."

"A compliment?" Will clutched his heart with his left hand before flicking the left turn signal to turn into the Magnolia Palace, as the voice from the GPS on his phone instructed.

"You're funny."

"I'm hoping you will get the chance to see I am a fun guy," Will said.

"What does it matter?"

Will slowed the vehicle down. "I am not crazy for thinking about the moment we first met at the elevator, Zoe."

"Well…" Zoe's voice was slow and hesitant. She chewed her bottom lip and cut her eyes toward the passenger-side window. "Maybe not completely crazy."

"How about I save you the trouble of trying to impress me with your work? I have major plans for Ravens Cosmetics and after our interview I believe your work is what I'm looking for. Why let our creative differences get in the way?" Will asked, and Zoe's mouth gaped open once again. A jolt of energy streamed through him. He was not his brothers, but he sure did sound like them. He didn't like the idea of mixing business and pleasure for a night or two. Will differed from his brothers that way. He wanted permanent, but was it possible Zoe was the one? "Okay, I'll back off. I'm the crazy person."

The tires crunched over the unpaved red clay driveway. Blooming magnolia trees lined the way up to the hotel.

"Please don't take this the wrong way," Zoe finally said. "But when I met you that morning, we probably could have made a go of things. Honestly, I thought you were a model and I was willing to give up my rule about dating clients."

"And now?"

Zoe shook her head from left to right. "Now, no way. You're going to be my boss."

"You don't have the job yet," Will said, raising his brows. He was turned on by her confidence.

"I will." Zoe sighed. "It was meant for me to work at Ravens Cosmetics."

"Oh, really now?" Will drawled and shook his head. "Did you see us together in your crystal ball?"

"The comedian again," Zoe retorted with a bored yawn. "I may tell you about it one day. Until I decide to share with you, you need to get used to the idea of us being nothing more than employer and employee."

That idea didn't appeal to Will. The hour and a half they'd been together already hadn't been enough. Maybe he should have flown into Atlanta to give them more time to get to know each other on the way down to Southwood. On the other hand, if by any miracle Will changed his mind about Zoe's work, they would end up working together. The last thing he needed was future tension between the two of them over a fling. With half the cousins tired of the business, and Donovan's trysts, Will didn't need the hassle. "Think you can at least settle on us being professional friends?"

There had been many times over the last month when Will resented having this CEO position. Now was one. But if Zoe only wanted to remain friends, he'd respect that. Hopefully there'd be plenty of cold water in this Magnolia Palace.

The Magnolia Palace sat on ten acres of lush green land, embraced by thick weeping willows in the back and strong magnolia trees that lined the paved circular driveway, which ended in front of the steps of the white plantation-style home. Four white columns reached from the wraparound porch to the second floor and up to where there seemed to be a balcony at the top of the roof. Someone stood at either of the long slit glass panes on both sides of the massive black double front doors.

It amazed Will how quickly the business mentality switched on in his mind. As a businessman realizing that the majority of his cosmetics were used in magazine editorial pieces, Will immediately thought this place would be the perfect background for a print layout. He scolded himself for thinking of work. Finally he understood what his parents meant by not letting it consume him. After seeing what the business did to his siblings, his father had tried to dissuade his children out of participating in the company. But it was in their blood. And when Will's brothers and sisters learned of their stake in the company, wild horses couldn't have kept them away. His parents might have sent him away to special soccer camps and facilities, but eventually, Will ended up at Ravens Cosmetics. And, yes, it was consuming his life. At least there was a bit of a break right now—sort of. He liked loud noise and the busy life. But he guessed for one week he'd be able to tough it out.

From the way his cousins described what his time in Southwood would be like, he'd assumed he would be stuck in a room watching pageants on television to get caught up. One look at the sprawling grounds and Will longed to stretch out in one of the hammocks and read a book. Although Will hated to admit it, he was looking forward to spending a week here and discovering all about the South. Even though Miami was in the south of Florida, it was not *the South*.

Relaxation called his name. As he thought about sleeping in, his attention turned toward the passenger

beside him who was wiggling in her seat with anticipation. How was he supposed to relax with her near
him? Hopefully she'd hang out with her friends and
stay out of his hair, although he fully expected her to
wear him down about his decision. Zoe was out of the
car before he placed the car in Park.

The massive doors of the B and B opened. Will expected a tuxedo-wearing butler to step out of the doors,
but instead, a tall African American woman with long
blond hair stepped onto the wraparound porch carrying
two mason jars of a brown iced beverage.

The moment the woman and Zoe locked eyes, Zoe
squealed and, out of the corner of his eye, he was sure
she pawed the ground like a bull and ran toward the
other woman. The woman turned to give the man
standing behind her the glasses and met Zoe at the
bottom step. The two embraced in a screaming hug.
Clearly they knew each other, Will thought to himself.
He'd grown up with sisters and knew how overly excited they were to see their friends. Will also knew it
was best to stand back and wait until the lovefest ended.
He clasped his hands behind his back and waited. The
man now holding the glasses stepped off the porch with
a chuckle and a shake of his head.

"I never get this kind of greeting when I come
home," he said, pushing one of the glasses into Will's
left hand.

The frosted glass cooled Will's palm. He stepped
forward and for a shake. "Will Ravens," he said.

"Hey, Will," said the man with the firm grip. "Stephen Reyes, husband of this squealing ball."

The squealing ceasing, the blonde woman stepped
to the side, and that's when Will noticed a very round

belly. Given the fact his sister had kids, Will guessed the woman was seven months along. She stood with her hand on her hip and glared at her husband. "Did you just call me a ball?"

"No, dear." Stephen winked before giving his wife his undivided attention. "Why would I say something like that?"

Zoe linked her arm with her friend's and dragged her over to where the two men stood. Stephen handed Zoe the other glass. "Will, this is one of my oldest friends, Lexi Pendergrass."

"Lexi Pendergrass *Reyes*," interjected Stephen with a dramatic roll of his *R*. "And why does she get to call you her oldest friend but I can't?"

"Because I know things." Zoe laughed. Will liked her laugh. It was light, bubbly and friendly. Zoe reached over and gave Stephen a hug. "As I was saying, this is Will Ravens."

Stephen leaned forward and whispered, loudly enough for Will to hear, "We'll have to have a real drink later, Zoe, so you can tell me what you know."

"Will Ravens?" Playfully, Lexi stepped between the pair and, instead of a handshake, gave Will a hug. "How on Earth did the two of you manage to arrive together?"

"I would have been here much later had Mr. Ravens not offered me a seat on his plane."

"The company's plane," Will clarified. "I spotted Miss Baldwin at the airport seconds before she was harassed by a…" He turned his attention to Zoe for a moment. "What would you call a wannabe LL Cool J?"

Zoe's eyes widened. A set of dimples popped up on her cheeks. "Exactly."

"Aren't you the superhero?" Stephen inquired with a humorous chuckle.

Lexi elbowed her husband in the ribs and kept talking to Will. "I cannot thank you enough for everything Ravens Cosmetics has done for the pageant. And for taking the time out of your schedule. I can't imagine coming into your position, you wanted to leave so quickly."

"Well, I'm sure you know how it is when Naomi and Joyce ask a favor," Will began with a chuckle. He took a sip of his beverage. The thick syrup coated his throat and he realized it was sweetened tea.

"Asked, or more or less forced you?" Lexi joked, hitting the nail on the head. "I know how they can be, so I have to apologize. I'm sure you're out of your element."

Beside him, Zoe snickered.

"I want to learn every nook and cranny of Ravens Cosmetics. If coming to your lovely city is one of the tasks, well, it's worth it." Will cleared his throat. "Besides, I'm always up for a challenge."

Lexi offered one last hug and pulled away. "Good. Let me show you guys to your rooms. Stephen's cousin just bought and renovated the place. I've got everyone working on the pageant sequestered here for the week, so I'm playing hostess today."

It was on the tip of his tongue to ask if that was necessary, but any words were lost as they followed Stephen and Lexi into the foyer of the Magnolia Palace. The black hardwood floors absorbed their footsteps. Adorning the walls were old pictures of a family—perhaps the people who originally owned the home. There were two large rooms, one on either side of the hallway. One appeared to be a sitting room, the other a library filled with shelves of leather-bound books. They traveled farther toward the wide-set staircase, which curled and broke off in two different directions. Light spilled in from the upstairs balcony over the crystal chandelier, creating a prism effect against the white walls.

Will's room was upstairs near the back of the house. The ceilings were high and the walls painted a pale blue. More portraits hung from the walls in gold frames. He went inside to decompress, but got caught up in the view from the balcony. The lush green backyard was neatly trimmed. A wooden path led to the docks, which jutted into the deep blue water of a round lake surrounded by more trees. Off to the side, on land, Will spotted a hammock and visualized himself in it with his shoes off and curled up with Zoe.

Will scolded himself for his obsession with Zoe. She'd made it clear she did not want to get involved with him. And she was right. Will needed to focus on the future of the company. He willed himself not to fall for the pretty smiles. Pretty faces were a dime a dozen and usually accompanied by a motive. Zoe was no different. Still, though, the confidence she'd exuded in the car was impressive as well as a turn-on.

This was not Will at all. He expected this lustful behavior from Marcus and Donovan. Will prided himself on being in control, but with Zoe, common sense went out the window. Did he dare hurt her feelings and let her know he did not see her in the future of Raven Cosmetics? Would it make her feel better to know he at least saw her in *his* future?

Thinking of her made him stiffen all over. He needed to splash some water over his face. Will moved over to the door he assumed would lead to the bathroom and yanked it open; a scream came from the other side. Upon further inspection he groaned. There stood Zoe with a fluffy blue-flowered towel wrapped around her silky dark brown skin. The sun filtering through the white-lace curtains highlighted the gold undertones of every curve.

"I guess Lexi forgot to mention the shared bathroom." Zoe recovered with an airy laugh.

Damn, this was going to be the longest week ever.

No amount of hot water could wash off the humiliation of her potential boss walking in on her almost naked body. How was she going to look him in the eyes now in a potential board meeting? After a disastrous moment before her after-travel shower, Zoe changed into black leggings and a black-and-white-checkered T-shirt long enough to cover her behind. She headed downstairs to the patio with her tablet in hand, hoping to take some amazing photographs of the setting sun. Because she and Will had gotten there early, the other guests hadn't arrived yet. Dinner was in an hour and a half, giving Zoe much-needed time to get reacquainted with the pier. She trotted barefoot across the grass to the dock, where the afternoon sun warmed the wooden planks.

Bright shades of orange, red and yellow smeared the horizon. With her breath caught in her throat, Zoe stood at the curve of the railing, in the same spot her father had knelt to propose to her mother. With the Magnolia Palace reopened, this would be the perfect spot for her father to re-propose to her mother. Zoe smiled at the horizon with excitement. She snapped a few pictures before deciding to return to the back porch.

The oversize white swings—and the fact that a producer friend had just sent her an advance copy of a superhero movie she'd worked on—helped put pep in her step. There was nothing better than the good people winning.

Zoe turned to head back to the porch, but she careened into a hard body. As she bounced backward with a prolific apology, the wooden rails creaked. The last thing she needed to do was fall into the water with her tablet. She hadn't even sent any of the files to her Cloud. She welcomed the strong arm around her waist and reached for the impeccably muscled arms.

"Whoa," a deep and now-familiar voice said into her ear.

"Mr. Ravens," Zoe gasped. Once her eyes began to focus, she narrowed in on his lopsided smirk.

"Let's see, we've shared a plane, shared a seat on a plane and I've walked in on you taking a shower."

Heat burned her cheeks. Zoe held her index finger up to stop and correct him. "Almost in the shower."

Will inclined his head. "Okay, almost. However, I do believe we are beyond the formalities. Please call me Will."

Zoe bit the right corner of her bottom lip. "Alright, Will. You have to call me Zoe."

"It's a pleasure, Zoe."

He had no idea what a pleasure it was to still be in his arms. Zoe cleared her throat. No matter what, she was going to be the Creative Design Director for Ravens Cosmetics. She needed to stop these romantic fantasies about her future boss. Taking a step away, Zoe waved her right arm at the water.

"What do you think of the view, Will?" Zoe asked with a shaky voice. "Beautiful, right?"

"You're absolutely right," Will said.

Out of the corner of her eye, she noticed he hadn't stopped looking at her. She bit her bottom lip again to keep from further blushing. The tactic didn't work and the heat from the sun was nothing compared to the flush on her face.

Will's brows rose, his left eye half winking. "Are you okay?"

"Oh, I'm fine," Zoe recovered quickly. "Were you just on an evening walk?"

"Sort of. I came to tell you your bags arrived."

"Thank you." Zoe breathed a sigh of relief. "Dare I ask how you managed that?" Zoe had been concerned about leaving her bags on the scheduled flight. But Will had said he'd take care of it and clearly he had. She'd expected to have her bags by tomorrow. This was better news. Zoe didn't like to be away from her makeup for too long.

"You don't want to know."

Zoe rolled her eyes and playfully pushed his biceps, hesitating for a moment at the way the muscle flexed. She wanted to keep her hand there, maybe let her fingers trail against his pecs, but that would be weird, especially since she'd made it clear they were not going to act on any impulse they may have. "Don't tell me you're going to have to take a pretty flight attendant out on a date all because of lil' ole me."

Why did she say that last line in her Southern belle accent? And, as her spine straightened, Zoe questioned her sanity. Did she seriously just curtsy? Judging from the strangled laugh escaping Will's throat, she guessed she did. "Sorry," Zoe coughed. "I don't know what's come over me."

"You're back home." Will provided an answer.

It wasn't the answer Zoe wanted to hear but she'd go with it. Better go with his than the naughty thoughts circling around in her mind.

"Well, thanks again for getting my bags to me."

"Not a problem," he answered.

They both started walking back toward the house. Zoe was well aware of how close they were to each other. Their forearms touched. Her fingers itched to link with his but she managed to control herself.

The only car parked off the circular driveway was the one they had driven down in. Lexi had left, as expected. She had her own home to tend to. From what Zoe gathered, Stephen's cousin had purchased the land and the Magnolia Palace and recently finished the remodeling—a job well done, Zoe thought to herself. But she had not seen the hotelier.

"Any sign of the rest of the guests?" Zoe asked.

"Stephen left to pick up someone just before I came outside. Are you starving? I'm sure I saw a basket of fruit on the kitchen table."

Zoe scrunched up her face. "I think I may have a bag of microwavable popcorn in one of my bags."

Now it was Will's turn to scrunch up his face. "Microwavable popcorn is not good for you."

"Are you telling me you happen to have popcorn kernels and an air machine in your bags?" Zoe teased, pushing his arm once more. Will's large frame didn't budge. "Leave me and my popcorn alone. I'm going to watch a movie."

"Yes," he said seriously. When her eyes shot up in

surprise, Will flashed a killer, million-watt smile. "Of course I'm kidding. What movie are you planning on watching?"

Zoe glanced down at her tablet. She preferred to keep her love of superheroes a secret. After getting teased in junior high school, Zoe learned to keep it to herself. On some websites, she'd never found anyone who shared her love but rather more or less mocked it. So she'd learned to stifle her love and watch in secret. "Oh, I did a makeup job a few years ago in college for a buddy of mine who ended up going off to the military. He finally finished putting this low-budget CGI film together and well, he sent me a copy."

They reached the back porch. Will pressed his hand against Zoe's lower back and guided her up the wide steps. Their strides matched. All too aware of the heat from his touch, Zoe prayed he didn't feel the sweat drizzling down her back.

"So, you're a movie makeup artist, as well?"

"I am extremely talented, Mr. Ravens. I can beat anyone's face," she said. Will stopped walking, clamping his hand on her shoulder. To most people, Zoe had to explain that beating a face meant putting on makeup. As CEO of a cosmetics company, he surely knew this information, which only meant his frown was for not using his given name. "Sorry, *Will*." Zoe shook her head and laughed.

"What do you mean, 'beat'?"

Zoe stood still on the top step. "You're not serious, are you?"

Will pointed his finger at her and let out a laugh. "Gotcha there."

A slow and unsure chuckle escaped Zoe's mouth.

For some reason, she didn't believe him. Was it possible for a CEO of a cosmetics company to not know what *beat* meant? In keeping up with the trends, someone should have taught Will the lingo. Maybe believing he didn't would ease her irritation at not landing the job right off the bat. Given he was going to be her boss one day, Zoe decided to take his word for it—for now.

"Why do I have a feeling I'm going to have to quiz you on cosmetics?" Zoe asked.

"What do I get when I get one hundred percent?"

With a roll of her eyes, Zoe laughed and shook her head. "Do we need to revisit our conversation in the car?"

"No, ma'am," Will said, holding his hands up in surrender.

Zoe moved over to the oversize swing. She patted the spot beside her. "Come sit. You can see my work in motion."

For the next half hour Zoe kept her tablet rested on Will's firm thigh while they watched the movie. Their breathing became synchronized and they laughed at all the right parts. A few "that's awesome work"s and "great job"s slipped out from the CEO. Zoe beamed. And then the part came where Zoe appeared on camera. She was just an extra painted in blue. The camera zoomed in on her and Will swiped his finger against the pause button.

"That's you."

"How did you know?" Zoe asked. In the film she wore a pair of yellow cat eyes.

Will's fingers pressed against her image on the screen. "I'd recognize those cheekbones anywhere."

"Nice eye," said Zoe, lips pressed together as she fought a smile.

"So, you're an actress, too?"

"Oh, no," Zoe said scooting away. "In truth, I knew this film was low-budget. It was a job for a friend, and in return I got to live out my dream to be a superhero." She covered her mouth, not believing she'd divulged her big secret.

Will turned in the bench to get a better look at her. "You're kidding me, right?"

"No, I'm not." Zoe stood up and covered her heart with her right hand and raised her left hand in the air. "I confess I am a superhero geek."

In surprise, Will stood up and took her left hand in his. He bowed his head and brought the back of her hand to his lips. Zoe's right hand moved from her heart to the back of her neck where she was beginning to sweat in this sweltering heat. "You're not going to laugh at me?"

"Laugh?" Will shook his head. "Hell, I might just ask you to marry me right here and now."

Chapter 4

The credits at the end of the film raced as fast as Will's heart had during the movie. Arms folded across his chest, Will spent the entire time trying not to make physical contact with Zoe in fear of her taking his failed attempt of a joke of a proposal too seriously. Zoe's stare, intent on her monitor, gave no indication. Will had battled himself internally. A marriage never survived on a mutual love for superheroes. His doubts of Zoe's ability to work at the company subsided, knowing about her penchant for good and evil—the epic battle in most comics. Spotting the evilness of his anti-cousins was a necessity. Will never played around with marriage. He'd managed to never lead on any soccer groupie with words implying a future with him. He planned to marry one day, just not today. Will's mild panic attack subsided with the arrival of the rest of the guests.

Lexi had made sure there were enough judges for her pageant. Will, the head of a major cosmetic company. There were two beauty queens, one former and one current. The guest celebrity judge was none other than infamous model Sasha Foxx, once a child actress, now a woman who'd grown up in front of the camera—and was someone all the men at Magnolia Palace seemed to have had a crush on at one time or another. Will was glad he wasn't the only male at this event. Kahlil Kane, heir to the Kane Diamonds empire, was serving as a judge, as well. Kahlil's family owned several high-end jewelry stores in Miami, New York City and LA.

The men bonded quickly with the new owner of Magnolia Palace, Ramon Torres, a cousin of Stephen's, over a few bottles of Torres Rum. It was nice to hang out with cousins who got along rather than fighting all the time and weren't in competition with each other. Will spent the evening in the study with the cousins instead of in the room right next door to Zoe. She was too much of a distraction and she'd made her intentions for their relationship—or lack of one—known.

Respecting what Zoe wanted was hard as hell, especially knowing she was perfect for him. How many other women who loved superheroes and knew more about the cosmetic business than him was Will going to come across who were as beautiful as Zoe? None.

So the price he had to pay for avoiding Zoe all evening long was a splitting hangover.

According to Lexi's itinerary, the judges were scheduled for a tour of the historic downtown area. With the pageant being held at the theater on the prop-

erty of Magnolia Palace, the contestants needed to re-
hearse without the judges around or spotting them on
their way to the theater next door. Since the contestants
were all local ladies from Southwood, housing was not
an issue. Lexi insisted her staff enjoy the Magnolia Palace. The tour got the officials out of the place so they
couldn't be accessed by the contestants or develop a
bias toward anyone in particular.

As he got ready for the day, Will tried to talk himself into being excited over the tour, but he could feel
the skepticism as he showered. Dressed in a pair of
khaki cargo shorts and a red-and-blue-striped polo,
Will thought of his family and headed out of his room.

Call him biased, but Will was partial to Overtown.
His great-great-grandparents had moved down south
to work on the railroads with industrialist Henry Fla-
gler. Back then, African Americans lived separately
from their white coworkers. Fanny Ravens, Will's
great-grandmother, had had the great insight to bottle her mother-in-law's products and travel to Miami
to sell them.

Where his grandparents were raised was a historic
city. Before the big highway boom, their successful
business had stood on West Second Avenue. Back in its
heyday, Will's great-grandparents opened their homes
to the women and men in their neighborhood. They offered a shave or beard trim for husbands and pin-curled
hairstyles paired with the perfect shade of red lipstick
for wives when they needed to get ready for picnics,
outings or even for events held at the Lyric Theater.
After World War II ended, many celebrities stayed at
the Mary Elizabeth Hotel. Knowing guests at the hotel
were going to need beauty supplies, Joe Ravens made

a deal to have their products in every room. A round of applause brought Will out of his stroll down memory lane.

Zoe stood in the center of a group, pressing the pad of her thumb against one woman's lips. "There you go," Zoe cooed. "Now you can go all day and drink whatever. I promise that lipstick won't smear."

"And my lashes won't smear against my eyelids." The woman pressed what looked like a spoon into Zoe's hand. "You're a genius, Zoe. Thanks for this beatdown," the woman said.

The terms women used for their makeup and outfits were violent. Beatdown? *There was that word again.* Will shook his head and tried to recall the woman's name. Mack, or Makenzie, or Kenty. She'd come in with Ramon and helped out with dinner and was friendly. Will remembered her mentioning that Lexi put her in charge.

"No problem, Kenzie." Zoe stepped back to admire the work she'd done. From the back, it appeared she wore a blue flowered sundress and a pair of blue flats.

"There you are, Will," Kenzie said, eyes wide and long lashes fluttering. "Would you like some coffee or breakfast before we leave for the tour?"

All eyes turned to Will. The women and men—members of the talent search, directors, the emcee, and various coordinators—waited for him to answer, as they clearly had been waiting for him to come downstairs all morning long. Shoulder bags were hiked up on the ladies' shoulders. The men not watching Kenzie were pacing.

"I'm fine," Will said, clearing his throat. "I apologize for keeping you waiting."

"You're good." Kenzie ambled over to him and grabbed him by the elbow. "We already paired off—except for Zoe, she was a little late, as well."

The rest of the group began to move out the doors while Zoe lingered behind. This morning Will had made sure to listen for noise in their joint bathroom so he wouldn't walk in on her. What had kept her lagging this morning? Will watched Zoe as he made his way to her, taking in the perfectly round bun at the top of her head. "So, you were late also? Hmm, did you oversleep?"

Zoe shrugged her shoulders and unapologetically said, "Never question a woman with perfect winged eyeliner about being late."

"I have no idea what you just said," Will admitted, smitten with her confident voice, "but it sounds nice." He kept his voice on an even keel and made a mental note of her vast experience, which reminded him to keep his mind and hands off Zoe.

Like she often did, Zoe gawked at him, leaving him feeling either the butt of an inside joke or worse, inferior. "And you're the CEO of Ravens Cosmetics?"

At headquarters, Eva and Dana bailed him out when it came to terminology. Naomi and Joyce prepped him with flash cards before big meetings. In Southwood he was on his own. A nervous chuckle escaped his throat. "I see I'm not going to get away with much with you. What was this beatdown you gave?"

"You're representing the company as one of the judges?"

Inadequacies washed over him. The pressure reminded him of his first penalty kick. Will had eventually gotten over it and he'd get over not knowing terms. He could learn. "I am."

"Well, you'll see my beatdown there." Zoe winked. Then she let him off the hook with a shake of her head. "Okay, fine, a beatdown is when a woman's makeup is flawless, which is what my work is. Your company's products and my skills…" She shook her head again, but this time let out a low whistle.

"Ravens Cosmetics has been sponsoring this pageant for a while now."

The corners of Zoe's lips tugged upward. "You guys donate a lot of materials."

"We do."

Zoe lifted a lavender tube with RC printed in gold. "Yes. And do you know what this is?"

Confident after remembering what Kenzie said, Will nodded. "Well, it's our famous lipstick line, Much Needed. You're holding Much Needed Nude, of course."

"I…" Zoe said as she pressed the tube against her chest. The dramatic effect was to possibly show her confidence, but all Will saw was the swell of her breasts underneath the dress. "*I* am what makes this lipstick famous. When I blend this nude with a shade from RC's Get line, Get Him Back, the deep, winey red mixed with nude gives it a blackberry color that makes for a sensual lip."

"Interesting use of our products." Will grinned when she nodded in approval. He admired her. "And that's a good reason to keep you around, isn't it."

"That, and you need my insight on what products and colors to keep. You guys discontinued this merlot color last year, so I make a mental note to check out all the beauty supply stores and drug stores in every town I'm working in to buy every tube I come across."

Another reason RC needed a Creative Design Director. He needed a better idea of what needed to stay and go. "Duly noted. Low sales of Get Him Back forced us to cut back on the product. But I like your concoction."

"You need to keep that in mind when you're going over your list of interviewees. What was I? Number six?" Zoe winked.

"Actually you're a ten," Will said as he wiggled his brows at her.

A horn sounded outside and her gold hoops jingled as she bobbed her head back and forth and said, "We need to get going before Kenzie has a fit."

"She scares me," said Will. He ambled down the steps and extended his elbow for Zoe to take.

Zoe accepted his gesture, wrapping her blue-polish-tipped fingers against his skin. An image popped into Will's mind, one of Zoe touching him this same way, only with her wearing a white dress and him a tuxedo.

"You should be scared of her. Kenzie used to be the head cheerleader for Southwood High. She is used to commanding large crowds of people to having spirit."

"Ah, Southwood High," Will joked. "Will we be visiting the school today on our tour?"

"Probably."

The bright sun accosted his eyes. Will blinked several times, and while he waited for his eyes to adjust, the sweet scent of blooming magnolias filled the air. When his eyes cleared, all the faces of the guests peered out the van's window at the two of them. He felt the flex of excitement when Zoe's hand twitched.

Ramon Torres stepped out of the driver's side and lifted his aviator glasses. "You folks are welcome to ride with us, but Will, man, I think with your height you might be a little uncomfortable in the back."

The last thing he wanted to do was make someone else switch seats. Will turned his head toward the spot where the Maserati sat parked under a magnolia tree. He turned back to Zoe. "You're familiar with the area in case we get lost while following them, right?"

There was a slight rise and fall of her breasts as Zoe gulped. "What?"

"How 'bout we follow you all?" Will asked Ramon, who sent a head nod as an answer.

So much for trying to keep his distance from Zoe, Will thought. "I hope your heart wasn't set on driving in the van."

Zoe chewed on her bottom lip before rolling her eyes. "Fine, but don't try that old trick of running out of gas on a country road."

The warm air filled his lungs when he took in a deep breath at the sight of her long legs in her dress as she wiggled away. "Yeah, well, so far *every* road around here is a country road."

"Cute," Zoe called over her shoulder.

Will took a few long strides and caught up with her before she reached the passenger's side of the car. "Let me get that for you," he said, leaning down. The motion brought him closer to her ear. He was sure the sweet magnolia smell came from Zoe.

"Thanks," she said, glancing up.

And he was supposed to stay away from her? Even if Zoe earned the title of CDD, Will wasn't sure he would be able to. She was intoxicating. He inhaled once more before closing the car door after she was secured inside. Will walked around the car to get to his spot. The engine purred to life and he maneuvered down the drive to catch up with the van.

While Zoe pointed out various historic sites, Will enjoyed listening to her speak. During the interview she'd been so poised and proper. Right now, the country air relaxed her. She smiled and his world lit up. At one point while they were driving, Will almost ran off the road watching Zoe pull her thick black hair loose from the bun at the top of her head.

She asked for the top to be put down so they could enjoy the morning sun. The women he usually dated did not appreciate the top being down. And the women he'd dated in the past did not sing along with the songs on the radio. Zoe sang absentmindedly and made no apology when she got half the lyrics wrong.

Entertained, he followed the van closely and they stopped for lunch at a local restaurant. During the tour, they passed the First Bank of Southwood, which Lexi's parents owned. Like many businesses in Overtown, businesses in Southwood had begun due to the lack of support from other places. Will and Zoe passed Lexi's shop, Grits and Glam Gowns, in front of which a crowd of girls lined the sidewalk. Strange, considering it was a school day.

A lush park across the street from the shop was filled with kids kicking around a large red ball. Plastic lined a baseball diamond so the kids could slide into the bases for a large game of kickball–Slip 'N Slide. They drove by the courthouse and the town square where, according to legend, Confederate and Union soldiers decided to stop fighting and live peacefully together. The town had its history, Will thought. The best part of the tour was Zoe. She was a natural spokesperson, something to consider for the job.

After putting the car in Park under a shady weeping willow, Will strolled over to his personal tour guide's side of the car to let her out.

"Thank you," Zoe said breathlessly.

"You okay?"

"I just realized I missed breakfast this morning and got a little lightheaded." Zoe swooned and Will wrapped his arms around her waist. The move was innocent enough, but touching her evoked so much temptation. She was ill, and here he was thinking about pinning her against the car and kissing her.

They stood, eyes locked. Zoe lightly pressed her hands against his chest. She wasn't pushing him away, though, and the urge to take her hand in his to kiss the palm or her fingertips overcame him. Will closed his fingers around her left hand and started to bring it to his lips.

Some of the guests from the van were spilling out, glancing in their direction. His brain switched to business mode. If Zoe got the job, this embrace might be misconstrued. If she didn't get the job, she could sue for sexual harassment. Will finally understood her dilemma.

"Are you okay now?" Will asked her, reluctantly letting her go.

With pink cheeks, Zoe nodded. "Thanks for not letting me fall," she said.

"Never. Now let's get us something to eat before you faint."

* * *

Seated across the table from the world's most handsome man, Zoe tried to concentrate on what the other guests at the table were talking about. Most of the people invited were a part of the team Lexi had put together to help design, build and judge the upcoming Miss Southwood Glitz Pageant. Miss South Georgia opted to stay behind with her mother.

A few people included Zoe and Will in their here-and-there conversations, but Zoe was intrigued with Will's story, especially when he told the table about his former soccer career last year. Lexi was right. She stood corrected on her thoughts of him being a workaholic. It sounded like his travels were equally balanced with work and fun. Why was he still single?

"Can you sue for someone ruining your career?" Zoe asked him after a waitress came and set down a bowl of fudge brownies smothered in homemade vanilla ice cream from The Scoop. She'd originally declined dessert after having the shrimp po' boy sandwich, but seeing it on Will's plate drew her in. Using his forearms, Will pushed the bowl toward her and caused a thin wrinkle in the linen tablecloth. Picking up an unused spoon, Zoe dug in.

"Accidents happen," Will explained. "I skated by for years with no injuries to my knees. Soccer is not dangerous as, let's say, football, but we all go into the sport understanding what injuries we might incur. And getting hurt is part of the job."

The fudge from the brownie coated Zoe's tongue. She closed her eyes and slowly rolled them to the back of her head. The satisfying taste threatened to steal her senses. When she opened her eyes, Will sat across from her, amused. A grin spread across his face.

"Is it good?"

"You ought to dig in." Zoe nodded. "The Scoop makes the freshest ice cream ever, and because there are no additives, it melts quickly."

"I'm trying," Will said, scooping up a combination of ice cream, brownie, fudge and a cherry.

Their spoons played hockey for a minute over the last cherry and Zoe realized she'd been greedy. "I'm sorry. You can have my cherry."

At that, Will sat back in his seat and gave a throaty laugh. Heat warmed her face when she realized what she'd said. "Oh, my God, grow up," she ordered while trying not to laugh at her choice of words.

"Alright, I'll try."

"So tell me more about you and soccer," Zoe asked, taking another bite. "You said you played in Germany. Do you miss it?"

"I did when I first came back, but I missed my family more."

The family. Zoe knew all about them. If she told him she'd done a school project on them, would it freak him out? "Are you and your siblings close? I've hung out with Donovan and Marcus before. I never knew they had another brother."

With a scoop of brownie on his spoon, Will nodded. "We are. Not as close growing up as I would have liked."

"No?" Zoe forgot about the dessert between them. She leaned forward to listen.

"No, my folks didn't want me to fall into the RC trap of being seduced by the money, and when a coach saw the soccer potential in me, my parents pounced on the opportunity to have me trained."

"What did that mean?"

"I went to a boarding school that concentrated on sports for athletes. You know, the kind with no distractions." Will lowered his eyes to Zoe's cleavage.

Zoe sat upward. "So, no girls?"

"None."

He probably became some wild child in college, Zoe thought. "What did you do for prom?"

"What's a prom?" Will asked, and before Zoe could complete her gasp, he winked. "I'm kidding. My brothers and sisters went. I saw the pictures."

"You never went to prom?"

"What'd he say?" Kenzie asked from her end of the table.

Zoe leaned forward again and craned her neck to look at Kenzie. "He said he never went to the prom."

One of the men, a photographer named Gianluca, or Luke, as everyone called him, shook his head with an audible *tsk*. "What?"

The other staff all began to tell their stories. Prom had been a rite of passage for a lot of the men at the table. Considering the direction of the conversation, Zoe wondered about Will even further.

"It's no big deal." Even though he shook his head, the red tint creeping across Will's high cheekbones said something different.

The conversation began to turn to everyone's attire for prom. Zoe mouthed an apology and Will winked as an acceptance.

"How was your prom?" Will asked.

"Oh. I didn't go to prom." Zoe beamed. "Comic-Con was going on that weekend in California."

"I commend your priorities." Will nodded his head. She figured he would understand. Part of what she loved about her job was that pairing the right shade of lipstick with the right woman could really have that woman feeling like she had superpowers.

"My mother was not happy. She forced me to attend this party in Diego Martin called a *gradz*. It's a Trinidadian version of a prom."

Will scooped up some of the ice cream. "What happened? Didn't win prom queen?"

"That would require a tiara and a gown. The school had neither. But we celebrated the end of the year together and that counts, right?"

"This is the saddest story I've ever heard," Kenzie added.

Kathleen Royal, judge and the former Ms. Wheelchair South Georgia, nodded. "I had the best time at my prom. The best date, too."

The two ladies clinked their glasses together and Zoe shook her head. She caught Will's eye again and her heart raced.

"Do you recall your date?"

Zoe felt the coy smile spread before she could stop it. Will caught it as well, and began to grin.

"Clearly you remember him all too well."

"Now, now," Zoe said, shaking her head. Was that a bit of jealousy in his voice? "It was so long ago."

"Not that long, I'm sure," said Will. "Go ahead and tell me about you and Mr. Gradz. Let me guess, you were crowned the gradz queen."

In order to not answer, Zoe ate another bit of

brownie with the cream. Before she could take another bite, Will pressed his spoon down on hers and
pinned the utensil against the white plate. "What?"
Zoe asked, batting her lashes.

"No more dessert until you tell me about Mr.
Gradz."

"Mr. Gradz," Zoe drawled out, "is doing just fine. I
had lunch with him just the other day in LA."

"You flew out to see him?"

Zoe snickered at the frown across Will's face. "I
flew out for a client's movie opening."

"Seriously?"

"I am a makeup artist, remember?"

Will shook his head as if he didn't believe her. "But
you had our interview the other day."

Out of pride, Zoe inhaled deeply. "Believe it or not,
I am in high demand. My job has me flying across the
country on a weekly basis."

"And I thought the life of an athlete kept me on the
road," said Will.

"Which is why I am looking for a permanent job."
Zoe bit her bottom lip. "Sorry, I didn't mean to make
that sound pitiful."

"No worries." Will's wink warmed her soul just as
it had outside the restaurant. She still couldn't get over
the fact she'd almost kissed him. Thank God he came
to his senses. "It must be nice for your job to give you
the ability to drop in on your exes."

Although she had no reason to explain further,
Zoe felt she needed to. "He and his wife are lovely
company."

"Wife, you say?" Will straightened up, then exhaled

a deep breath and his shoulders slumped. "That makes me feel better."

"About?"

"Never mind," Will mumbled and went back to the dessert. "Tell me how you got started in cosmetology."

Zoe licked some fudge off her bottom lip. "You have sisters, right?"

"I do, a set of twins."

"Did they ever use doll heads to practice fake makeup and hair?"

Will nodded. "I believe they each got dolls for Christmas."

"Well, I got one for Christmas as well, and by the following year I'd gone through at least twenty-five of them."

"I understand the doll's face is washable," said Will. He set his spoon down on the edge of the plate.

"They are, but after I got in trouble for using all of my mom's, I created my own makeup with food and crayons and used it on a few of them, and didn't know how to make it washable."

"Wait." Will pressed his hand on the table. "You made your own makeup as a kid?"

Didn't he read anything on her résumé? "I did get a Bachelor of Science in biochemistry and an MS in Cosmetic Chemistry." Zoe rolled her eyes. "I'd like to think my childhood products inspired the first vegan products."

"You believe in vegan products over animal-tested?" Will asked.

Didn't he know anything about cosmetology?

"I'm sure your mother was impressed and mortified. I'm imagining the ants and the smells from your food-based makeup."

A memory of her grandmother came to mind. She rarely shared personal stories, but something about being in her hometown was nostalgic. "My grandmother came to my rescue. She was so impressed with the way I perfected the 1940s eye that she brought me more doll heads and encouraged me to do everything under the sun in cosmetology, how a product is made, applied and sold."

Will shifted uncomfortably in his seat and Zoe chalked it up to their meals. They had eaten a lot this morning from a food truck. Zoe figured he would burn the meal off with the walking tour of the history of downtown Southwood later after lunch.

"Okay, so you've always loved makeup."

"I love pretty things," Zoe responded.

In his response to her, Will wiggled his brows. "What do you know? We're very similar."

It was on the tip of her tongue to remind Will she wanted him to be her boss, and that this flirting, no matter how exciting, was inappropriate. But, truthfully, she enjoyed it. She loved the thrill he gave her with each cocky grin.

"Alright, y'all—" Kenzie clapped her hands together "—it's time we get moving."

Saved by the Southern belle.

The tour ended just before dusk. Will parked the sports car in the same spot and, like earlier, came to Zoe's side of the vehicle to help her out. His Southern manners were in rare form, Zoe thought, as she watched him move in front of the hood of the car. Despite setting her own ground rules, she couldn't ignore the wave of excitement each time she got the chance to be alone with him. She'd be lying if she said she was looking forward to the barbecue this evening. It meant she'd have to share his company with the other guests and right now jealousy tingled her senses.

She'd noticed a hairstylist batting her lashes at Will after dinner. A jealous bug did bite her, but she ignored it. Zoe had an agenda. And, so far, she thought she was winning Will's favor. They stopped by Grits and Glam Gowns, and Zoe was able to point out the jobs she'd done in the photographs hanging from Lexi's walls. Will didn't say anything about her work, but he did nod his head in approval.

Zoe didn't care for Rebecca Smith, who was half trotting and half limping in her four-inch heels toward the car. Who wore heels like that on a walking tour?

A few years ago, Zoe and Titus had been at the same show. In most fashion shows, makeup was done first and then the model went over to the hairstylist. The designer collaborated with her crew to create the looks she wanted for each model. One of Zoe's models needed more attention. Titus, irritated at not getting more of the intricate work, spent his time backstage gossiping with Rebecca, who held the models in line for hair. With Zoe's models backed up and Titus's models ready, Titus had received the high praise for being professional. Rebecca never mentioned the true reason for the holdup.

"There you are, Will," Rebecca exclaimed breathlessly. Rebecca's attempt at wing-tip eyeliner was shaky at best, and in the sweltering heat, the liquid had also leaked onto her upper lid. Poor thing was oblivious. Zoe was almost tempted to pull her aside and let her know. "I was hoping to find you before we ate dinner."

Will extended his hand to help Zoe out of the car and kept a possessive hold on her hand as he spoke to Rebecca. "You found us," he said, with an emphasis on the *us*.

Rebecca gave Zoe a tight-lipped smile. Zoe dipped her head to hide her sarcastic grin. "I wanted to talk business with you."

Zoe disentangled herself from Will's grasp. "You two go on ahead. I'm going to change for the cookout." She excused herself and walked through the yard, through the hickory-scented air. What business did Rebecca have with Ravens Cosmetics? Zoe didn't realize she was stomping up the steps until Lexi, cuddled up on the hanging swing with her husband, glanced up and paused her conversation. Zoe waved an apology and headed upstairs. She had no business feeling any way over Rebecca. More than likely the hairstylist just wanted to be a part of RC, much like Zoe did. Who could knock her for trying?

Inside her room, Zoe debated whether or not to shower and erred on the side of caution. Being sweaty and standing near the lake water was a good way to get bitten by a mosquito. She slipped out of her sundress, padded barefoot into the bathroom and locked the door to Will's side of the room, just in case Will decided to do the same. Once in the shower, scrubbing her body with a loofah, Zoe thought more about what Rebecca and Will were talking about. She was in a sudsy lather and her mild rage grew as her mind wandered. What if Rebecca wanted the CDD position? What if Rebecca was willing to compromise her integrity? There was no what-if, Zoe thought bitterly.

Zoe got out of the shower, dressed in a pair of denim shorts and red crop top, and stomped down the stairs in her red flip-flops, already in a tizzy. Will stood by the grill, nursing a bottled beer, talking and watching Ramon maneuver a grilled chicken leg over to its other side. When he finished, Stephen stepped in with a basting brush and brushed a thick, deep-red sauce over the meat. Will nodded his head in approval.

"That's what I'm talking about," Will cheered the barbecuers.

"Oh, brother," Zoe groaned, walking over to them.

Kenzie came out of nowhere and linked her arm with Zoe's. "Men will bond over anything, from a sports show to meat."

"Not just meat, woman," Ramon said, puffing his chest and lifting his hands out to the sides. "We made fire." To celebrate Ramon's feat, Will and Stephen gave him high fives.

Zoe liked this side of Will. He wasn't as stuffy as he was with his brothers at Ravens Cosmetics, where he had to be the boss. He was himself…or, at least, she thought so. "What's on the grill?"

"I have some chicken now," said Ramon, "and there are burgers and hot dogs keeping warm in the oven."

"So, we're ready to eat?" asked Kenzie.

Ramon looked at the grill and nodded. "Yeah, let's start calling the guests down."

"Is there anything I can help with?" Zoe asked. "I learned from my grandmother that if I didn't bring anything to the party, the least I can do is help out."

"Yours, too, huh?" Will chuckled. "We may end up washing dishes together tonight."

Great, Zoe groaned inwardly, *a night of getting wet with Will.*

Chapter 5

The following morning, a wave of nerves washed over Zoe when she brushed her knuckles against the door to Will's room. She'd dressed in a pair of comfortable red workout shorts, a plain white T-shirt and some running shoes, and stepped out of her room into the hall to go right next door. She heard no movement but in a second Will opened the door.

Before leaving her room, Zoe had prepared a speech to coerce him into going off Lexi's daily schedule. Then he answered the door in a pair of black basketball shorts with the waistband hanging low on his hips, exposing those V-shaped muscles. Zoe's mouth went dry. She'd figured he was fine, but damn.

And the last thing she'd expected to find on his defined chest were the initials TOP over his heart. A woman? Zoe stamped down the surge of jealousy coursing through her veins.

"Hey," Will said, cocking his head to the side to catch her attention.

Zoe hadn't realized she was staring until her neck ached as she straightened it to meet his gaze. "Oh," Zoe began, "I, uh, I wanted to see if you wanted to go off course again today."

"You have something in mind?" Will asked and reached up for the top of the door frame. A natural bulge formed in his biceps. A natural moan threatened in the back of Zoe's throat.

"I thought you'd like to visit the Four Points Park today for a workout."

"A park?" A spark of excitement was in his voice.

"Well, yesterday you almost killed us while driving because you seemed so distracted by the view," Zoe teased.

Will began to rock back and forth, his arms still holding the top of the door frame. Now all Zoe could see was the way the muscles in his legs flexed. She gulped once more. Was he doing this on purpose?

"What was I doing yesterday?" Will asked.

Zoe blinked back up to make eye contact with her potential boss. If she kept saying that in her head, she'd eventually believe it. "I should have asked how your forehead was doing, considering how many times you hit your head against the window every time you saw a green pasture."

"Whatever." Will chuckled and pushed himself away from the door. "Well, all I need to do is put on my shoes and we can head out."

"And a shirt," Zoe reminded him.

From the middle of the room, Will turned around and winked. "Too much for you to handle?"

Playfully Zoe rolled her eyes and scoffed. Without stepping into his private sanctuary, she stood in the doorway and leaned against the jamb. "Whatever, I'd hate for your virginal skin to be attacked by the Southern mosquitoes—they're unlike any bug you've ever come across."

Will sat on the edge of his bed and slipped on a pair of black tennis shoes. The crumpled blankets on his king-size bed created images in Zoe's mind that she needn't think about. When he finished with his shoes, Will stood to his full six-four height. He reached for something in the covers, then stood and slipped a black T-shirt over his beautiful body. Zoe swallowed her disappointment.

"I can promise you one thing, babe," Will said. "Nothing about me has been virginal in a long time."

The only thing Zoe could do after a comment like that was choke on her words. "I wasn't talking about that."

"I know." Will crossed the hardwood floor, grabbed something off the dresser against the wall and then stood so close to her in the door frame that Zoe felt his heartbeat thump against his chest. "But I was."

At first, Zoe assumed Will was being boorish and using his size to push her out of the way. So she turned to the side with her back against the frame. Will turned to face her, and her heart raced. He lowered his lashes and licked his lips as he stared down at her. It was barely after eight in the morning and Zoe was already working up a sweat. This wasn't fair.

"Do you mind?" she asked him, hoping he'd catch on to her sarcastic tone.

"Hey, you're the one who didn't move."

In true dramatic form, Zoe sighed and took a big step to the left and into the hallway. "Better?"

"Not really," Will mumbled with a wink. "So, where are we going again?"

"To the Four Points Park."

A set of keys jingled in the palm of his hand and scraped against the brass knob when Will closed the door behind him with one hand. He placed his other hand on Zoe's lower back. She tried not to be skittish and willed herself to remain calm.

"You're dressed like you're going to work out," Will observed.

"I need to." Zoe nodded. "You keep shoving your desserts at me."

"Yeah." Will laughed. "I ordered one and you pulled it toward you."

"You pushed it toward me like you wanted to share!" Zoe gasped.

"Uh, no." Will shook his head. "I was making elbow room and getting ready to dig in when you assaulted my dessert with your spoon."

Done with this version of the truth, Zoe folded her arms across her chest and sighed.

"Then let's talk about last night and the triple-crust peach cobbler with the homemade vanilla ice cream." Will patted his stomach. "Or, at least, I believe it was homemade. I barely got some."

In jest, Zoe rubbed her belly and offered a lazy smile. "Oh, it was homemade, and it was good, too."

"So you admit you stole my dessert?"

"I was helping you out," Zoe argued. "Both desserts were too large for one person to eat. You really should be thanking me."

Bowing at the waist, Will nodded. "You're right, and thank you," he conceded. "But you must know, I'll share anything with you."

They walked along the hallway together and down the stairs. A lighting director and his assistant were the only ones awake and preparing their breakfasts. Silver-domed trays were spread out along the dining room's buffet. Fresh fruit in clear bowls stood as the centerpiece on the table. Zoe stepped in for a moment to snag two bananas before she followed Will out the door. Even though she didn't need help down the steps, Zoe wouldn't have minded Will's gentle touch again. She bit the inside of her cheek to avoid showing any emotion.

Will proved to have a good memory. They drove without her having to give any directions. The banter over who'd eaten how much dessert continued until a song from a female group Zoe had once worked with came on the radio. Without thinking, she turned the volume up and began belting out the punk-rock lyrics. At a red light, Will slowed the car and the song began to fade away. Zoe remembered her surroundings and bit the nail of her index finger.

"Sorry." She grinned.

"Don't be sorry." Will shrugged, a smile spreading across his face. "Is the band a favorite of yours?"

"In a way," said Zoe. "I did their makeup for one of their album covers. You may have seen it in my portfolio." Zoe glanced over in time to catch his fingers gripping the steering wheel.

Will cocked his head to the side. "Can we be honest here?"

"Sure."

"I wasn't a fan of your work."

The light may have turned green, but Zoe ceased to notice everything else around her. Her heart slammed against her rib cage. "What?"

Will shrugged. "You said I could be honest."

"Well, I didn't mean rip my heart out and slam it on the ground," Zoe shot back quickly. "We're talking about my life's work."

"Your work is stuck in the eighties."

"It's not stuck in the eighties," Zoe gasped. "It's an homage to the eighties. It's my signature."

"Big hair, bright colors, crazy colors." Will shook his head and frowned. "Not my cup of tea, but fortunately for you, I don't have the final say in the hiring. We do have to put it to a vote."

"And do you want to tell me what my odds are right now?"

Chuckling, Will reached over and patted Zoe's shoulder. "I have no desire to be that honest with you."

They drove along a few more miles before reaching the park. Will slipped the car into an empty spot with no cars on either side and stepped out. Zoe was still at a loss for words. He didn't like her work and he had no problem telling her so. So why *wasn't* she ready to rip his head off?

In the beauty business, there was always competition. If Zoe had a fit every time she didn't get a job, she'd be one miserable person. The only time she hated being passed over was when it came to Titus. He stole everything from her. Zoe swallowed down the bubbling irritation. No need to worry. Zoe had Donovan, Marcus and the twins on her side. Surely that was enough, right?

"Thanks," Zoe said, taking his hand as he offered to help her out. "I mean, for being honest."

Will held on to her hand to press it against his heart. "Can I be honest with you some more?"

Butterflies puttered around in her belly. How much honesty was she supposed to take in one day? "How about, if you beat me around the field," Zoe pulled herself away and took off running, "you can say whatever you want."

"No fair!" Will shouted at her backside as she left him in the dust.

Cute. She wanted to race. Will had two choices. The competitive side of him wanted to, of course, win this instant race, but winning might cause more hurt feelings than Will wanted to provide. Even though Zoe smiled at him after he gave his honest opinion, Will knew better than to push his luck. So, clearly, the other option was to let her win.

Going with that, Will jogged behind Zoe. She had great form, knees up, feet up as she paced herself. His steps were quiet, quiet enough that when he turned around to run backward alongside of her, Zoe jumped off to the side with a little scream. Her pace became a full-on dash. The light laugh she made, as if she couldn't catch her breath, was infectious. As Will caught her laugh, he made the mistake of closing his eyes and not watching where he was going. Thanks to his carelessness, he tripped over a log and fell down to the grass in a laughing heap.

"Will!" Zoe screeched and came running back. She slid into him like he was home plate. "Are you okay?"

"I'm fine," Will hooted. In truth, his pride hurt, but

as long as Zoe's hands roamed his body he wasn't going to admit anything. The damn clothes were in the way.

In a caring manner, Zoe sat and cradled Will's head in her lap. "Seriously, what were you thinking?"

"I wasn't," Will groaned. "I was just trying to make things interesting."

"Ouch." Zoe's eyes and mouth became pinched. Suddenly Will's head hit the ground as Zoe rolled onto her back. Puffs of dirt and blades of grass flew into the air when Will scrambled to her side. "Cramp. Cramp."

"Relax," Will ordered. The way Zoe grabbed the back of her right thigh, Will knew exactly what hurt and what to do. He moved her body to lie flat and wedged himself between her legs. With his right hand he lifted her right leg, his thumb grazing down her calf, roaming behind her knee; with his body, he pressed her thigh toward her. "How does this feel?"

"It hurts," Zoe whined. "I think I broke something."

"You didn't break anything. Breathe through it." His face hovered over hers and her sweet breath blew across his face. "You got this."

The way her eyes squinted at the corners did something to the blood in his head. It fueled his body. Will blinked and focused on Zoe's face. For a makeup artist, she wore very little. And yet she still radiated beauty. Zoe winced once more. Will encouraged her, stroking the hard muscle against her femur. He nearly buckled when her body melted in his arms and a moan of satisfaction oozed from her parted lips.

Zoe inhaled into the stretch. The more limber she became, the closer Will's face came to hers. He leaned his body forward and somewhere in the move Zoe's leg slipped from his hand and wrapped around his waist.

Will placed his hands in the grass on either side of her head. Once more Zoe's lips parted; this time, she arched her back toward his frame. Her eyes focused on his mouth, and with the closeness of their bodies, the pitter-patter of her heart slammed against his chest. This was it. This was going to be the moment they put their business aside. He felt it. She felt it. They both wanted it.

A pair of hummingbirds buzzed in the air in front of them. At the sound of a high-pitched whistle the birds flew off. A black-and-white soccer ball sped by them and chasing it was a group of teenage boys. Will sprang to his feet, bringing Zoe with him. He nudged Zoe behind him so the boys did not catch sight of her disheveled clothes but kept hold of her hand.

"Boys, boys," began a man with a whistle dangling from his neck and a clipboard in his hands. He wore a pair of red coach's shorts and a white T-shirt with the initials SHS across the front. A red visor shielded his freckled face from the blistering sun. "Watch where you're going. You almost knocked these people down." The man jogged to them and apologized, then backed up. "Holy crap! You're Will Ravens."

"Guilty as charged." Will extended his free hand for the coach.

"Jesus, it's a pleasure to meet you," said the man. "My name is Barney, Barney Chatman. I'm such a fan of yours."

Behind him, Zoe made some noise and stepped forward. "A fan, you say?"

Barney nodded his head eagerly and pumped Will's hand. "Am I ever. I followed your career at Stanford."

"Stanford," Zoe said, her interest piqued, and the corners of her mouth turned down.

This tidbit of information didn't need to be shared right now. Not when he was trying so hard to prove he was a regular guy. Regular guys attended regular colleges, not universities competing with Ivy League schools. Will didn't consider himself as privileged as his cousins. He'd worked hard to earn everything he had.

"And, of course, in Germany when you were with the Teufels. I was in Germany your second year with them and got the chance to watch a match."

"Thanks," Will said. "It's great meeting people who know the sport."

"Well, not like you." Barney stepped back and held up his hands in surrender. "I can't believe I've got you standing here. I can't believe my boys just ran right by you without recognizing you and paying their respects."

Will waved off the honor. "When I was young, the only thing I saw in front of me was a ball."

Barney's thick brows rose. "You don't think…could I interest you in checking out the boys? I mean, they'd really get a kick out of meeting you."

A gentle nudge from Zoe dug into his back when he looked to her for permission. "Go on and do, like, a scrimmage thing with them," Zoe encouraged him.

"You're better?" Barney asked, inclining his head toward Will's ankle.

Not wanting to appear weak in front of Zoe, Will straightened to his full height and nodded with confidence. He was. He'd recuperated. Of course, his days of playing professionally were over, but where was the harm in running around on the field with a few high school students?

"I'm not sure," said Will. "My friend and I were just getting started working out."

Another elbow, this time in the ribs, and Zoe wiggled her brows. "I'm injured, remember?" To emphasize her pain, Zoe limped in a circle. "Besides, you've seen my work. Let me see yours."

"Ravens Cosmetics is my work," Will reminded her, tipping the edge of his index finger across the slope of her nose. He offered a smile when she rolled her eyes toward the single puffy cloud in the blue sky. "But I'll go just so you can see how I give everything one hundred percent."

"Oh, man, this is the best," Barney exclaimed. He patted Will on the back of the arm. "Let me go tell the boys."

Zoe laughed as they headed for the field. Some of the boys were stretching, while others were bouncing a ball on their knees back and forth to each other. Will hated to admit he was excited to kick the ball around. He'd been far younger than these kids when a coach spotted his potential. High school was nothing but academics and sports. Judging from some teenage girls gathering on the sidelines, Will predicted a healthy balance for these high school stars.

Blood pounded in Will's ears as he came closer to the field. His heart raced with deep beats. A ref's whistle blew, signaling the start of a match. The sound evoked the auditory memory of his rapid breath when he used to run full speed toward the soccer ball. He also recalled the deafening sound at the Raiders Stadium when his opponent's cleat had sliced into his flesh. The joy he felt overshadowed the pain. This was his element. He knew everything about the game. No one questioned him on the field. No one made him lose focus. Until now.

Since it was his fault that Zoe had to sit in the silver bleachers, the least he could do was try to make it comfortable for her. He ripped off his shirt, folded it and created a comfy spot for her to sit. Will had to admit her little curtsy in thanks was cute.

"Don't hurt yourself out there," Zoe called as he trotted off to join the crowd of boys.

On a soccer field, even a makeshift one, Will always gave a hundred percent, just as he'd promised to Zoe. Every now and then, though, he did glance up to where Zoe sat and smiled. Back in the day, Will had liked to think of himself as a sports-focused man. Of course, pretty women hung on the rails and even the sidelines to catch his attention, but Will had always been focused. He'd prided himself on that. Now, distracted by Zoe, one of the kids was able to steal the ball from him.

The players were fun and energetic. He was surprised at how many kids enjoyed soccer these days. A crowd of spectators began to fill the bleachers. At one point, Will shaded his eyes to make sure Zoe was okay. He spotted her becoming the center of attention of a group of girls more intent on whatever she was saying than the actual practice. The back of his hand dripped with sweat. He hadn't realized he'd been playing that hard. He didn't even have his cleats.

The sun was high in the sky, shining brightly over the entire park, by the time practice ended. Folks from Magnolia Palace gathered around the edge of the field.

His newfound friends, Ramon and Stephen, clapped. All the boys hung around, begging for an autograph. Will signed soccer balls, T-shirts and even a pair of shoes.

But the only thing Will wanted to do was run over and swing Zoe in the air. This was the first time since the accident that he'd felt a complete fit on the field. He realized he owed it to Zoe. It had been his fear of looking bad in front of her that inspired him to keep up with the younger crowd.

The bleachers were filled with a young crowd of students, all of them holding their cell phone devices. So he held off from swinging Zoe around. Knowing how quickly things spread on the internet, Will wondered what Eva or Dana or the twins would think—or even the board for that matter. With her as a candidate for Creative Design Director, physical contact was not a good idea. It was clear Zoe wanted the position and he didn't want to jeopardize everyone else's opinion of her. Knowing where they both stood. She wanted the job Will did not want to give her. Yes, she showed signs of potential but she lacked the back-to-basics approach he needed. Will risked a sexual harrassment lawsuit with potential witnesses for Zoe.

Zoe stepped down to the bottom bleacher. Will held his hand to help her transition to the ground. Her arms stretched in the air to wrap around his neck but Will took a step back and instead raised his hand for a high five. Her brows rose in question, and Will nodded at the teenagers.

"We have an audience," he whispered into her ear, and she half turned to see where he motioned to.

Understanding, Zoe nodded her head and cleared

her throat. Their hands met in a midair high five. "I'll make sure to tell the board their CEO is a true team player."

The idea of Zoe being on his team was intriguing. But Will had to stick to his guns and make a thorough examination of all the candidates. It wasn't fair to the others that he got to spend this time with her. If he did decide to hire Zoe, there'd be rumbles from other people. The only thing he hoped was that Zoe would still want to see him after the final decision was made. If Zoe cared about the company, she would understand, right? Dare he risk sticking by his guts? Turning her down now either opened or closed the door for them to potentially date. She might try to brush it off, but there was something between them neither one of them could deny.

"Thanks for talking to us, Miss Zoe."

Thank God for the perfect timing of Lexi's niece. Kimber Reyes tapped Zoe on the shoulder, innocently interrupting a series of naughty thoughts going off in Zoe's head. Zoe took a giant step backward and away from Will's hot, sweaty body. She fanned herself with one hand and tossed him the shirt he'd allowed her to sit on with the other.

"Oh, Kimber, it was nothing," Zoe said, ignoring Will's penetrating curious glance.

"I'm going to go home and try it."

"Try what?" Will asked.

As hard as Zoe tried to will Kimber to stay strong and not fall for the dazzling smile Will flashed, it didn't work. With the game over, Zoe appreciated the modest attempt Will took to cover up his muscles. He tugged his shirt over his head. "Zoe was just teaching us a few techniques for our makeup by mixing glitter in with our gloss."

"You're stunningly beautiful," Will said to Kimber, which only made the child giggle hysterically. "Good job, Zoe."

Kimber shook her head. "No, not right now. For our pre-prom pictures we're going to take tomorrow."

"I'm so excited for you." Kenzie came over and hugged Kimber's shoulders. "You're a shoo-in to win." She tugged the side ponytail Kimber sported. "This head was made to wear the Southwood High Prom Queen crown."

Forgetting she was in the company of Will, Zoe participated in the pre-celebration, holding Kenzie and Kimber's hands to jump around and squeal. Their commotion brought over the other men from the Magnolia Palace. Everyone sobered when Stephen cleared his throat like the overprotective guardian he was. Zoe admired him and his brother Nate. They'd moved to Southwood soon after their other brother, Kimber's father, passed away in a car accident along with her mother. Immediately, they'd acclimated to the small town and both men found longtime residents to fall in love with. Zoe craned her neck to see if she could spot Nate Reyes around here somewhere. No such luck.

"Whoever heard of prom pictures the day before prom?" Stephen scowled. "When I was growing up, we took pictures the day of."

"And risk getting your dress messed up?" Kimber cringed and rolled her eyes. "No, thank you."

The uncle and niece duo could go on for hours about

their views of the world without intervention. "Where's Lexi?" Zoe asked Stephen.

Stephen groaned and shook his head. "She's on bed rest."

"Bed rest?" Zoe gasped.

Kimber huffed. "She's fine. It's Tío Stephen who is forcing Lexi to stay home in bed."

Relieved, Zoe sighed. "Did something happen to worry you?"

Patting his niece on the shoulder, Stephen shook his head. "She's been so involved with this pageant she forgot to take her prenatal vitamin yesterday."

"According to Lexi," Kenzie offered, whispering not so softly behind her hand, "she got as far as the door before he freaked out."

It was easy to imagine Stephen being so careful where Lexi was concerned. He loved her deeply and, of course, Lexi was madly in love with him. They made Zoe long for a relationship where she could settle down. For some reason, Zoe glanced over and found Will staring at her. Her heart fluttered.

Clearing her throat, Zoe tore her gaze from Will's back to Stephen. "You promise she's okay? I know she is nearing the end of her pregnancy."

"She's fine." Stephen nodded. "Feel free to stop by this evening."

"We have dinner planned for everyone tonight, don't we, Ramon?" Kenzie leaned forward to include Stephen's quiet cousin in on the conversation.

In an uncomfortable fashion, Ramon scratched at the back of his head. "I think I forgot to take it out of the freezer."

"Are you serious?"

Before they had a chance to get involved in the wrath, Zoe grabbed Will's arm and waved goodbye to Kimber and Stephen.

"I did tell you she scared me," Will said, once they were out of earshot.

"I'm scared for Ramon," Zoe laughed. "Maybe we shouldn't have left him."

Will stopped in his tracks. For a moment, Zoe wondered if he wanted to go back and rescue his new friend. He paused and looked over the hill. "Nah, I think he'll be okay."

They began to walk together in silence. Zoe wasn't sure where they were going; she just knew she didn't want to share Will with anyone right away.

"How was playing soccer again for you?" she asked when they reached the other end of the shallow lake. Their knuckles brushed against each other as she walked on the higher part of the leaf-strewn path beside the water. "Want to go back to it?"

"Not a chance." Will sighed. "I know I may not be as experienced in the makeup world as you, but there's something about doing this job for my grandmother that makes me feel honorable."

"Your grandmother, huh?"

"Yes. I promise you, I am my grandmother's favorite grandchild."

Zoe felt her lips stretch across her face as she tried to hide her smile. What would he say if he found out she did a school project on the family and never came across him? Of course, she'd done it a long time ago. "You don't say."

"Why do you sound surprised?"

"Surprised that you were spoiled by your grandmother?" Zoe made a grand gesture toward her heart. "My bad. How could I ever think such a thing?"

"You sound like my cousins."

Water rushed by an open drainage. A few birds scattered to the top of the skyscraper-tall pine trees at the sound of their footsteps. It was the perfect afternoon for a romantic stroll. *If there was a romance between us.*

"Is that a good thing or a bad thing?"

"Have you met all of my cousins?"

Zoe ticked off the cousins she knew. She was closest to the twins. "Isn't that enough?"

"There are more, and all of them are leery of me as the CEO."

"Didn't you say they nominated you for the job?"

Will nodded and hung his head. She hadn't realized he'd picked up a blade of grass until he started picking it apart. "They did. It was more an attempt to see me fail. Christmas is great in our family." He half chuckled as she mewed out a pity *aw*. "Don't feel sorry for me. At least the other group of my cousins, the loyal ones, want me to succeed, which I plan to do half out of spite."

"If you fail," Zoe breathed, "Ravens Cosmetics fails."

"Exactly." Will stopped walking and offered Zoe a half smile. "Which is why it is imperative that I choose right for the next position. I don't want to let my grandmother down."

"You won't fail if you choose me."

Chapter 6

After a family-style dinner at the table, the men cleared the table and did the dishes. Their reward was another bottle of rum. Will needed it. Though his body was tired from the exercise, his mind raced after his afternoon with Zoe and their near kiss. Lips had never been so soft. Every dream he'd had last night was of the promise of how good he and Zoe would be together. But Zoe had made herself clear she wanted to be a part of Ravens Cosmetics. The more time he spent around her, the clearer it became to Will that he wanted to be a part of Zoe.

Everything came down to the Creative Design Director position. From what he'd seen, Zoe's work still did not pop to him. The work Will had seen—not just in her portfolio but also album covers for musicians and rap artists—was more for shock value. The bold colors and designs could have been considered art. Will liked to see a woman who looked like a woman, not a walking art gallery. Will thought of the Get line. The product titles were catchy—Get Him, Get Him Back and Get Revenge—but at the end of the day, vintage colors, such as bold red, soft pinks and basic nudes, stood the test of time; meanwhile, a majority of the trendy products were discontinued and in his opinion, a waste of time and money. Will recalled old photographs of his relatives over the years in their dresses and makeup. They started off with vintage red lipstick and natural eyebrows; as the family members grew, they experimented with the trends from the seventies, from heavy, bright blue lids and oversize lashes to funky colors, then the grunge fad, and eventually returned to the basic "less is more." Zoe was a trend. He wanted classic. How was he supposed to have both?

She was *haute couture.* He smiled at his use of the phrase. Dana would be so proud of him. In just a few short weeks he'd grown. He recognized the names of the Ravens Cosmetics Zoe left in the bathroom and ignored the competitors' products.

The sleek black cell phone on the nightstand by his bed lit up. It was the first time all week it had rung. Will expected to see Marcus's or Donovan's face on the screen, but instead it was his sister. Speak of the devil. He smiled just the same. "Hey," he said, accepting the FaceTime call.

Like all of the women in the Ravens family, Dana was extremely beautiful. She'd begged their parents to allow her to be part of an RC back-to-school runway show, and her modeling career had taken off at the age of thirteen. Now, at almost forty, with three kids of her own, Dana was still as beautiful as ever.

"Hey, little bro," Dana said with a bright smile. From her position, Will could tell she was seated at the utility table in her kitchen. A bowl of fresh fruit sat on the island bar behind her and the refrigerator door opened and closed without a head bobbing over the countertop. One of the kids was sneaking their own snack. Will kept that tidbit of information to himself. "How is the country life treating you?"

"Bad news spreads fast," Will said.

"I wouldn't say bad news, more like gossip." A crash from another room sounded and distracted Dana for a moment. "Tell me about Southwood. Are you wearing overalls yet?"

"I haven't gotten that sucked in yet." Will laughed as he said it, but the small town was growing on him. The walk around the lake had sold him, or maybe it was the company he kept.

Dana narrowed her eyes and leaned in close to the screen. "You sound and look relaxed compared to the last time I spoke with you."

"It was just last week that we spoke, and that was after I had to tell a room full of interviewees that we're going to have to get back with them about the job interviews that I was late to, thanks to Dixon."

Nodding, Dana rubbed her chin. "I heard Titus was in the running. He's worked a few shows I walked in."

If his memory served him correctly, Titus was the six-foot-five artist from the interviews. Truth be told, out of everyone in the pile, Will had preferred Titus's body of work. Women looked like women, not art. On top of being a great makeup artist, Titus being a man in a female-dominated field made it fresh and new. The idea of hurting Zoe didn't sit well with Will, though.

"He is."

"And what about Zoe Baldwin? The twins told me she's at the pageant."

Will rubbed his hand over his mouth to cover the smile that the mere thought of Zoe evoked in him. "She's talented."

"And very beautiful," Dana added.

Secrecy was never at the forefront for the Ravens family. Will shook his head and sighed. "Okay, what did Donovan say to you?"

"It wasn't just Donovan," Dana said. "Marcus picked up on some sexual chemistry between you two."

"Marcus and Donovan? Our brothers who both have issues with dating women from the office?"

Another crash came from behind Dana. It sounded like a bowl with a thousand Legos falling. Judging from the way Dana rolled her eyes, Will guessed he was right. She squinted her eyes, as if pushing the noise out of her mind. "Will, they say the tension was so thick between you two. Are you sure it's wise to be working with her in a secluded town?"

Considering the way they were interrupted every time he and Zoe got close, the last thing Will would call Southwood was secluded. Someone was always around. The thought of his time with Zoe being put in jeopardy didn't sit right with Will. He sat up further and shook his head. "There's nothing going on between us."

"Are you sure? Because after going over the video surveillance from the downstairs lobby—"

"What?" Will pinched the bridge of his nose. "I

see Jerraud is taking advantage of his position at the building."

"It's not a position," Dana corrected her younger brother. "It is his job. He runs Anderson Securities and part of that requires putting out any fires at Kelly Towers."

"There was no threat."

Dana shook her head back and forth. "Judging from the heat rising between you and Miss Baldwin from the minute you two laid eyes on each other, I'd beg to differ."

Jesus, he'd forgotten about the security cameras on all the floors. He shouldn't have overlooked the sneaky lengths his sisters would go through in order to get some information on him. "So, this is how you get your gossip?" Will had to laugh. He shook his head. "You're scoping out surveillance tapes."

"Whatever, William. This isn't about me. This is about you and Zoe."

"There is no me and Zoe," Will snapped and when he did, he heard an unmistakable sneeze from the other side of the bathroom door. A jolt charged his system. While it was Zoe's idea to keep things friendly between them, he still did not want her to think he wasn't attracted to her. He desired Zoe. Will scratched the space above his heart where his TΦP, Tau Phi Rho, tattoo rested. The ink reminded him he needed to get back in touch with Dominic at some point this week. He felt bad for being in his frat brother's new hometown and not hanging out with him at any point.

"I would hate for her not to get chosen and then want to bring a lawsuit on RC. That's all the cousins need to hear before they decide to cash in their chips."

The door to Zoe's room slammed shut and footsteps shuffled down the stairs. Will cursed under his breath. "I've got this, Dana. Okay?"

"Fine. Well, I better get off this thing before the kids destroy my house."

After they said farewell, Will glanced at the itinerary on the nightstand to decide what to wear tomorrow for Lexi's last supper before the pageant Sunday. There was nothing formal until Saturday night and that was just a dinner. Since they were touring more old buildings, Will slipped into a pair of jeans, a Miami T-shirt and a pair of wheat Timberlands. He doubted they'd do a lot of running, but if they had to walk through the park or anything, Will wanted his feet protected.

Even though he knew Zoe had left her bedroom, Will knocked on the door to the bathroom they shared and opened it. The first scent was intoxicating. Magnolias. He grinned at the bottles of hair products with the Ravens Cosmetics label and wondered which ones she used. Whoever came up with the scent needed a raise. Will would never look at or smell magnolias again without thinking of Zoe.

Will understood Ravens Cosmetics, as a cosmetic conglomerate, was parent to several subsidiaries. The internet made it possible for consumers to try every product created under their umbrella. Years ago, it had helped sales skyrocket; now, beauty bloggers helped, too, but anyone with a camera phone considered themselves professional video bloggers, or vloggers, as they were known. Last Christmas, RC came out with a holiday mascara—Merry-Merry Mascara—and a customer with a cell phone reported her dislike for the makeup. Then someone purchased a tube but didn't care for the customer service she'd received and trashed the mascara. That video went viral. The bad press didn't help when the consumer named RC's competition as a better alternative. Some of these products seemed to taunt Will as he stood in the bathroom. The other products on the counter irked him. MDMFlow, PNK Digger and AJ Crimson were scattered on the countertop. Was it crazy to wish the only thing Zoe used on her body came from him or his company?

He saw a piece of jewelry Zoe wore every day. Using his index finger, he traced the hoop earring a few times, then pinched it to pick it up. Returning it to her would give him an excuse to see her—touch her, even.

Downstairs, he found Zoe seated at the head of the breakfast table draining a glass of orange juice. Though the glass covered her face, Will still caught her eyes watching him as he crossed the room. He bit the inside of his cheek trying to keep from flashing a smile at her. It seemed every time he did she would blush, and with a table filled with other guests working the pageant this Sunday, Will figured he needed to curb his flirting. What Dana had said resonated with him. He needed to keep to himself for the rest of the time here.

Kenzie carried on a light conversation with the group at the table. She kept directing the topic toward Zoe. Will snagged a biscuit and sat at the opposite end of the table from her. A silver bowl of honey butter sat in front of him. While he slathered the butter on his bread, he could only think about doing the same thing to Zoe. Her slender neck was exposed in her low-cut V-neck T-shirt with a witty picture of sparkling red lips on the front.

"Are you ready for today?"

Will turned to his left to find Rebecca sliding into the empty seat. She reached out with her right hand to stroke his forearm. Nodding, Will sat back in his chair and pulled the napkin from under his plate to wipe his hands.

"Of course," Will said. "I look forward to discovering more of Southwood's hidden charms."

"I can't wait to look at the old building," said Luke. He was the photographer for the pageant, but Will had also seen several freelance jobs he'd done for RC's digital spreads.

Will nodded his head in agreement. In one bite he consumed half of his biscuit. From across the table, Zoe stared and pressed her lips together. They'd almost shared a kiss yesterday afternoon.

Zoe had left with the girl named Kimber to check on Lexi last evening. She hadn't returned to her room until late. Will had been tempted to "accidentally" walk in on her when she was taking a shower, but he'd decided against it. Will wanted to talk about their episode yesterday.

They had been about to kiss.

He hated not being honest with Dana. In truth, he wasn't sure where he stood with Zoe. Zoe had more aspirations in life than being the wife of an athlete. Will liked the way Zoe took time to talk to the girls at the park. There were times he'd witnessed a grown woman push a child out of the way in order to get his autograph. Will could try to keep things professional like he promised his sister. The words he'd said to Dana weren't true. There *was* something going on between him and Zoe. It was only a matter of time. Because of his dedication and traveling with soccer, Will had never thought twice about getting involved in a serious re-lationship, yet when it came to Zoe, he wrestled with everything. Once the decision about the job was made, Will could concentrate on pursuing Zoe. Since she was from the islands, he knew the perfect place to take her on their first date when they returned to Miami.

"Alright, is everyone here who wants to go on the road trip?" Kenzie asked in her typically cheerful voice.

A chorus of yeses came from the Magnolia Palace occupants. Will looked forward to the van being over-crowded again. It would give him a chance to drive in the Maserati with Zoe. Alone.

"Okay," Kenzie went on, "Zoe, how about you sit up front with me and I'll drive."

Wait, what? Will thought quickly. This was his chance to have her alone. For a brief moment he con-templated banging his fist on the table or kicking the chair's leg in protest. But he was the CEO of a major cosmetics company. He was here on business to rep-resent said company, but he was fighting the urge to act like a spoiled child for not getting his way. Will started to get up, but a set of hands clamped down on his shoulders. Ramon was standing behind him.

"I kind of need a favor from you, bruh," his new friend said. He slid into the seat Rebecca had left. "Kenzie is a bit upset with me and has kicked me off the tour. I figured since you have an empty seat in that car of yours, I could catch a ride."

"Sure, not a problem."

Will didn't ask what the problem was. As with he and Zoe, there was clear tension between the former cheerleader and the owner of the bed-and-breakfast.

Zoe and Kenzie were already at the doorway. Both ladies glanced back and purposely tilted their chins in the air at the men before turning fully around and leaving.

Whatever Ramon had done to piss off Kenzie, he needed to stop. This was interrupting Will and Zoe's time together.

When the van pulled up to the Mas Beauty School, Zoe's heart started fluttering. She led the tour of her great-grandmother's beloved three-story structure. They started with the old classrooms on the first floor, where the original structure was made up of four rooms. The home started off as a single level and thanks to success, they'd expanded. Sadie Baldwin used one room for teaching, and she and her husband lived in another, raised their two boys in the other, and opened their third bedroom to students coming from across the state of Georgia, and even farther away, to study the techniques of the trade.

The success of the beauty school had made it easier for the Baldwins to add on to the house. The structure grew upward with two more stories. Sadie, whom Zoe called GiGi for short whenever she came to stay, had been quite young when she gave birth to Zoe's grandfather.

Zoe retold the story of the success of the original beauty school, and pointed out that two of the other downstairs rooms were turned into classrooms, as well. During the fifties and sixties, word had gotten out about Mas, and girls traveled from as far as Chicago to come to the school where the young student's parents and grandparents attended Annie Malone's as Poro Agents. Before the internet, businesswomen signed on as Poro Agents and sold Miss Annie's products. Miss Annie went on to become a millionaire and came out with her own hair-care line for African American women in the 1900s. GiGi molded her career after Miss Annie to sell to those who could not afford to travel upstate. It was GiGi's classes that had inspired Zoe to get a degree in cosmetic chemistry.

Zoe smiled at everyone soaking in the history lesson. A lot of the women were already aware of it. Even Rebecca nodded her head with awe. Old newspaper clippings about the accomplishments of all the graduates hung in frames, and a significant number of the former students had gone on to work at Ravens Cosmetics—a little bit of news clearly interesting to Will.

Will rubbed his square jaw with his hand and stood at one of the silver-framed photographs. The picture was of GiGi with the young and successful Naomi Ravens. When girls graduated from Mas, many went back home to start their own shops and salons, but GiGi thought those who went on to Ravens Cosmetics were the ones who truly succeeded.

The tour continued through the kitchen, where GiGi once used to stand at the stove and make sure all of her students were fed and taken care of. Eventually, when the funds permitted it, she had been able to hire a cook. By the time Zoe came to live here, the number of students enrolled had begun to dwindle. With more beauty schools popping up in so many different cities, no one needed to travel to get the hands-on experience GiGi gave. At one point, everyone in Southwood came to GiGi's school for free hair and makeup treatments at the end of each semester. After the doors to the school closed, GiGi kept her shop open for local customers until the day she passed away.

A rope draped from one staircase railing to the other, warning everyone away from the third floor. That was Zoe's sanctuary. Her father still lived upstairs when he wasn't gallivanting around the world to meet up with her mother. It was probably for the best. There'd be no telling what her old room looked like now.

Kenzie took over the rest of the tour, mainly guiding everyone back downstairs and outside to the second add-on to the home. In her typically excited way, Kenzie told everyone about the back area facing into the woods known as the Firefly Forest. The covered area was meant for cookouts and party events. Kenzie and Lexi had arranged for a special late dinner the next night. It was Lexi's way of thanking everyone for their hard work. Sunday was the beauty pageant and everyone was going to be torn in different directions.

Zoe lingered behind the group, mainly to keep an eye out for Will. She hadn't meant to avoid him that morning, it just sort of happened. Not finding him in the crowd worried her a bit. Somehow she knew she'd find him on the third floor. She ducked under the tape and trotted up the steps. Of course he was standing in her bedroom with the door open. His arms were crossed over his chest; he stroked the hair on his chin and stared at the wall. In his jeans and Timberland boots he looked more like a star on a trendy hip-hop reality TV show.

"The tape over the stairwell didn't clue you in that this area was off-limits?" Zoe asked, approaching. Years ago, when her father had opened the house for tourists, the carpets were taken out and the floors stripped to reveal the original hardwood. He must have learned his lesson after having them constantly cleaned. Her father also kept the off-limits sign up to keep the family's personal belongings safe. Kenzie had a key to the house, as the town historian did with just about every historic place in town open for tours.

"I like to pick and choose when the rules suit me." Will chuckled. He dropped his hands and nodded toward the wall. "Why didn't you tell me about this?"

Walking farther into the room, Zoe found her old canopy bed still intact. The creamy veils surrounding the bed were open and held back with eggshell-colored ties. The walls were a soft beige; off-white frames holding old family photos hung on the bare wall, along with a corkboard with the framed A+ paper she'd done on the Ravens family.

Embarrassed, Zoe closed her bedroom door before another rogue tourist strayed upstairs to witness her adolescent obsession. She stood in front of Will, as if her height could actually make a difference. Not a chance. "Don't look at that."

"Why not? I want to learn about my family history." Will gently moved Zoe to the side and moved closer to the report. Zoe waved her hands in front of his face. "Wait, is this the crystal ball you were talking about that told you you belonged at Ravens Cosmetics?"

Of all the times to remember something. Zoe groaned inwardly.

"I must say, I'm quite impressed," Will continued. "You managed to include my all of my aunts and uncles, including Aunt Octavia. Most people forget about her."

"How can they forget?" Zoe gawked "Before social media, she had to have been the scandal of the decade. I mean, the eighties were a breath away from social media. Can you imagine what the rumors would have been like? From what I read, no one could believe someone could walk away like she did and disappear." As Zoe went on, Will's lips flattened together. Zoe covered her mouth and shook her head. "I'm sorry. That was probably insensitive of me."

"Nah." Will let her off with an easy smile. "Everyone else in the family seems to have forgotten about the missing heir—she's been missing for a few decades now. My siblings and my cousins never knew her. We only know her as the abstaining vote."

"She still has a stake in the company?" Zoe asked.

Will nodded. "My grandmother…"

"Ms. Naomi," Zoe provided with excitement, pointing to the spot on the Ravens family tree, where an old photograph of his grandmother was pasted.

"Yes, my grandmother Naomi still believes Octavia will come back one day."

In a way, Zoe had always thought the same thing, especially with the way everyone used some form of social media platform. Didn't Octavia want to see her family? What drove her away? Zoe had a thousand and one questions.

Will brushed his elbow against her shoulder. "Look here, you got as far as my third great-grandfather."

Zoe beamed proudly for a moment. "Well, my great-grandmother swore by the products your family used to come up with and urged everyone to work for your grandmother once her students graduated." Then Zoe moved away, turning so he didn't see her blush. How much of a stalker did she seem right now? All her life she'd wanted to be a part of Ravens Cosmetics. "You must think I'm crazy."

"We've spent the whole week together, practically day in and day out. Why didn't you tell me about your family's links with mine?" Will asked. His voice neared her. Chills rolled down her spine. "Can't you see that's yet another thing we have in common? From what I learned today, it's as if our grandmothers aligned us to be together."

"Get serious," Zoe said as she spun around. She came face-to-face with his chest, which she stared at rather than meet his eyes. But it was useless. Will tipped her chin so she'd face him. "Will," she pleaded. "I heard you this morning on the phone with whomever. You said so yourself, there is no me and you."

"That was my sister Dana on the phone," Will replied softly. "If I gave my family any information about my love life, they'd plan a wedding before we return to Miami."

Strong hands brushed against the backs of her arms. Will's thumbs drew circles on her skin. She shivered and leaned against him.

"You're what's stopping what's happening between us, Zoe, because of one specific thing," Will said against her neck. "But you're overlooking the thousands of things we have in common with each other. You don't find that too often in two people."

Zoe bit her bottom lip and tried to fight her desires. At what point did she let go of her dream of being a part of Ravens Cosmetics? And at what point did she need to realize and give in to the temptations of the man who made her remember she was still a woman with desires? Everything about Will screamed he was the perfect man for her. She'd put all of her dating options on hold. None of the men she'd dated matched her need for success. After listening to Will's concerns with RC, she knew without a doubt they were perfect together.

Giving in, Zoe turned and found herself in Will's embrace. He cocked his head to the side and brought his lips close to hers. They'd almost kissed yesterday. The desire for a taste of him still lingered on her lips. Will finally put her out of any misery, satisfying her with a brush of his mouth against hers. A soft kiss greeted her at first, and then another one. In unison their mouths parted and their tongues danced together.

If heaven had a taste or feeling, this would be it. Will wrapped his arms around Zoe's waist and held her close as he deepened his kiss. Lost for a moment, Zoe gave in to every urge racing through her body. Her hands followed the deep muscles of his chest and wound around his neck. The tips of her fingers played with the curly hair at the nape of his neck. Will's hands roamed up and down her back, one bracing her shoulders, the other caressing her backside. Long fingers played with the hem of her shorts. The mere touch liquefied her.

A mew escaped Zoe's throat. Any common sense went out the window. The two of them found her bed and the old cushions absorbed their weight. Zoe lay beneath him, the palms of her hands embracing his face.

Will pulled his face away for a moment. His lips pressed against the curve of her collarbone and trailed along the edge of her collar. Her breasts swelled and ached for his mouth, not just the warmth of his breath.

"Will," Zoe moaned.

"Zoe," Will replied, trailing kisses back to her neck, jaw and lips.

"Zoe?" Another voice penetrated the barrier of the door.

Using all the strength she had, Zoe sat up straight. Will sat on the edge of her bed with a bewildered look on his handsome face. "Dad?" Zoe called out, and Will mouthed the same but with more questions on his face.

The brass oval door handle turned and creaked. The whole entrance took a mere few seconds, but in Zoe's mind it took forever for the door to reveal her father standing in the doorway while she struggled to sit up in the bed.

Because of the nontraditional way Zoe's parents had lived, with her having no stereotypical mom and dad to come home to every night, her maternal grandparents had been ashamed of their marriage. Zoe never wanted to do anything to cause her father embarrassment. All her life, she'd been the doting daughter. She never got in trouble in school. She went on with college and got her degrees, all without incident.

"What are you doing in here?" Frank Baldwin asked, his eyes narrowing at the sliver of space between herself and Will. "With a boy, no less?"

Zoe stood up. A cool breeze brushed against the exposed skin of her stomach. Quickly she tugged the material down. "Daddy, what are *you* doing here?"

"I thought I lived here." Frank folded his arms across his chest. "What are you doing here? Besides the obvious."

"Sir," Will said, bravely stepping forward with an extended hand. "My apologies for what you walked in on. I have nothing but the utmost respect for your daughter."

How embarrassing it was to be caught making out with a male by your father. But her father's inspection of Will's extended hand took the cake. Zoe grabbed her father's hand and pushed it at Will. "Daddy, this is Will Ravens."

"Ravens?" Frank repeated.

"Ravens," Zoe said in a clipped tone, knowing exactly where her father was about to go with this. His thick dark brows rose with curiosity and his black eyes darted between the two of them. "The Ravens family?"

"The same one on the school report." Will chuckled and pulled at her father's hand. "We were just discussing the lengthy research she did."

"Yes," Frank said drily, "because that's exactly what it looked like."

"Daddy," Zoe hissed. "Will is a guest."

"He was certainly making himself at home."

"I meant no disrespect, sir," said Will. "I got carried away and took advantage of Zoe's hospitality."

Frank eyed Will skeptically. Zoe waited for what seemed like forever for him to say something. "Zoe," he finally said, "go downstairs and let me and Mr. Ravens have a little chat."

Even though she hadn't been grounded in years, Zoe knew better than to argue with her father. She cast a pitiful glance back at Will, who winked at her. Funny how he wasn't nervous at all. The last time Zoe had had a boy in her bedroom, Frank used the kid like a punching bag found downtown at South-paw Shaw's Gym.

"I'll meet you downstairs," Will assured her.

"We'll meet you downstairs," her father restated.

"I really came into town to finalize things for the re-enactment of my summer engagement," Frank Baldwin said, pacing back and forth in Zoe's bedroom. "I'm not sure if Zoe ever shared with you, but Magnolia Palace is where I proposed to her mother. We're still married but these things keep the spark, especially since we don't live together."

Of course Will remembered the story and the place. "Yes, sir." Will nodded, trying to focus on Zoe's father.

"No need to get all official with the 'sir' business. Call me Frank. It was kind of refreshing, knowing my daughter is not consumed with work all the time."

Never in Will's life had he ever come face-to-face with a girl's father. Sure, he'd done the proverbial sneaking out of dorm rooms back in the day. But Frank Baldwin walking in on them almost took the cake. What did take the cake was Frank shaking Will's hand and thanking him for getting Zoe out of her comfort zone.

"Excuse me, sir?" Will leaned close to make sure he'd heard correctly. "I mean Frank."

Frank Baldwin folded his arms across his chest. "Don't get me wrong. I didn't enjoy catching her being pawed all over. But it was refreshing to see Zoe act reckless. My daughter has been insanely career-driven for a while." Frank fanned his hand toward the family tree. "As you can see for yourself, she's been a fan of the Ravens."

Will held his hands in the air. "I apologize. What you saw was just a momentary lapse in judgment. I truly respect your daughter and I hold her work in high regard."

"So you're hiring her for your company and you'll be keeping your hands off her?"

There went the whole hiring matter. Uncomfortable at being faced with Zoe's father, Will cleared his throat. "I am considering it. The decision isn't final."

"I don't understand," said Frank. He crossed the room to the white-and-pink desk.

"I've already spoken with Zoe." Will explained the situation with the board.

"You can't lose if you go with Zoe."

Those words resonated with Will as the two of them headed downstairs. Will liked that her father had decorated the upstairs hallway with framed photographs of Zoe's work. If she hadn't become a makeup artist, she should have been an artist.

The rest of the group was outside, but Zoe was seated at the large wooden table in the kitchen. Her eyes darted nervously between Will and Frank. As her lips parted to say something, the sound of a song by the late Prince sounded from Zoe's cell phone.

"Hey, Lexi." Zoe's concerned look washed away. "Calm down. What? Okay, sure, I can be there in a few minutes."

After she hung up, Will stepped forward, Frank close behind. "Is everything okay?"

"There's a slight emergency at Lexi's shop. Dad, is your car here?"

Frank shook his head. "It's at the new garage downtown. I took an Uber today."

Will's chest swelled with pride with the chance to save the day. "I drove here. I can take you wherever you need to go."

Chapter 7

Driving through the quaint little neighborhood only reminded Zoe of the life she wanted. Children played on their neatly manicured green lawns. Husbands washed their cars in the late afternoon. Smoke billowed from lit grills in the backyards. A faint smell of hot dogs on coal filled the air.

With the car's top down, Zoe heard the unmistakable splash of people in the pools behind the homes, as well. This was so different from what Zoe saw from her condo balcony every day. There were no lawns where she lived, unless you counted the sprinkle of green nestling under the sign with the name of her building. The beaches were always covered in half-naked men and women. Tanned bodies stretched on oversize towels or beach chairs. At every corner there was always a party going on.

"What's that smile all about?" Will asked Zoe. Of the four cars at the stop sign, Will appeared to be the only experienced driver. Pimply faced boys on the left and the right of them gunned their engines, and a girl with headgear was directly across from them. All three drivers had older males, whom Zoe assumed were their fathers, seated in the passenger's seats and pointing at the stop sign. Will, being last at the stop, waited. In Miami, she would have been gone by now.

Watching the fathers with their children reminded her of her father. Zoe glanced back at Will. "Care to tell me what you and my dad were talking about?"

Will inhaled deeply, contemplating her question, and then let out his breath. "I can't. Does that negate whether or not you'll tell me what's on your mind?"

"Have you ever thought about looking for Octavia?"

"You're seriously thinking about Ravens?"

Zoe shrugged her shoulders. "When am I not?"

"I appreciate your dedication to the family," Will said. "But for the record, my grandmother looked for Octavia for years after she disappeared."

"Does anyone know why she left?"

Will shook his head. "Not to my knowledge."

"So no one even knows if she's dead or alive."

Will blew out a long breath. "No. I wish for my grandmother's sake that she would make contact with someone from the family."

"I bet anyone in the family would be interested in hearing from her," Zoe commented.

"What do you mean?"

"Well, you said there's a divide between you and your cousins, whether or not to close the company doors. Her vote could help."

"Or hurt," Will said with a nod. "So was my family really what brought that beautiful smile to your face? If so, I might need to consider keeping you around more."

"You need to keep me around because I'm what's best for Ravens Cosmetics."

"There you go. Now, why don't you tell me what else was on your mind. Are you worried about what your father said to me?"

Knowing how persuasive Frank Baldwin could be, Zoe shrugged her shoulders. "I was thinking about home."

"Miami home or here in Southwood?" asked Will.

"No," Zoe answered. "I was thinking about my place in Miami."

"Yes, your Miami address," Will nodded. "I am going to need to know that information."

It was on her résumé, but Zoe decided not to bring her future at RC up right now. They'd crossed the threshold of any work relationship they might have again just then when Will reached over and squeezed her thigh. She bit her lip to fight back the excitement. Where would things have gone between them had they not been interrupted in her bedroom? One thing was for sure, Zoe's insides were awakened and she couldn't wait to have another chance of seeing where things would lead. "I live at the Cozier Condominiums."

Will let out a long whistle and began driving again. "Swanky."

After all the teasing she'd given him about growing up privileged. "Be quiet. I am leasing it from a former client."

"Someone famous?"

Zoe shook her head again and glanced at the view.

The condo was leased to her by the Ruiz family. Natalia Ruiz was a famous reality star who grew up in the limelight. When she and her family were in Miami, she always contracted Zoe. On several occasions Natalia flew Zoe out on location for special events. But after Natalia got married, she'd shied away from the cameras. Zoe knew where Natalia lived, but she'd never betray Natalia's trust. "You must know I'm not at liberty to say."

"Perhaps you will tell me over dinner Monday night."

"Monday?" Zoe repeated.

"I figured by the time we returned Sunday after the pageant, it might be too late. Although I could try to use my, what is it you say? My influence?"

"Affluence," Zoe corrected him.

"Yeah, that's it. I can call in a few favors and see about getting Trudy's to open."

Zoe turned in her seat and placed her hands on her hips. "What do you know about Trudy's?"

"What?" Will's mouth gaped open. "It's only the best place to get roti in Miami."

As much as Zoe loved her Southern food with its savory greens, crispy fried chicken and thick, sweet tea, she missed the taste of the Caribbean. "I might just let you take me there."

"When we return home, you are coming with me, or I will pick it up and we'll eat at my place or yours."

A chill of desire ran down her spine. "You're lucky their *gulab jamun* is my kryptonite."

The reference to a superhero didn't fall on deaf ears. Will winked and shook his head. "You should try the pudding made up with sweet dough," he said. "If you're good, I'll make it for you."

Butterflies fluttered in Zoe's belly. She looked forward to holding Will to his word. She looked forward to a lot of things with him. Seeing him naked and finishing what they started this afternoon was at the top of her list. "Turn left up here. It's the house with the bars on the upstairs windows."

"Bars?" Will's right brow rose with curiosity.

"It's a long story," Zoe laughed lightly. "But that sweet kid you met at the park, Kimber, gave her uncles a run for their money when they came to live here."

If it weren't for Kimber, Lexi and Stephen might not have met. Kimber had taken a very seductive dress from Lexi's store without permission, and Stephen—assuming his niece was innocent—had arrived at Lexi's store to give her a piece of his mind. Seeing how they were about to start a family of their own, so much for that plan.

Like the rest of the homes, children were playing on Lexi's manicured lawn. Philly, Stephen's younger niece and a seven-year-old future beauty queen, ran around the front yard, tiara secured on top of her twin pigtails as she shot a pink Nerf gun at two boys. Her army, a set of twins, stood by her side. The mini-militia stopped and saluted Zoe and Will as they pulled into the driveway.

Lexi stood at the doorway, her hairstyle looking bigger than ever, if it were possible. Her signature blond hair was pulled into a ponytail at the top of her head, which she shook feverishly. "I'm so glad you came. I have no idea how this happened so quickly."

Zoe got out of the car before Will put the vehicle in Park. "Where is the patient?"

"She's locked herself in the downstairs bathroom.

I don't think she even noticed while she was getting ready—until she looked in the mirror," Lexi said, crossing her arms together and biting her fingernails.

"You guys must have florescent lights," said Zoe. "Didn't I tell you to get softer ones in the bathrooms?"

"I'm not the one who needs to be convinced." Lexi turned back and gravely nodded. "It's also motion censored in case the patient tries to sneak in late. The whole house lights up inside."

"Did she say 'patient'?" Will asked. He slammed his door shut and started to follow them inside. Before he locked the doors, Zoe reached into the backseat for her caboodle. Will jogged around the car and took hold of it.

"Let me get that for you."

"Will, I've been lugging that thing around for years now." Zoe tried yanking it from his hands but he held on tight.

"Well, I haven't been around for years. I am carrying it."

"My hero," Zoe mumbled with a sly grin.

Fortunately for Zoe, she'd brought her emergency bag with her in the van when she left this morning with Kenzie and the rest of the guests. The pink case rarely left Zoe's side. It contained everything she needed to handle emergency situations, from waterproof mascara remover and a Ravens Cosmetics product perfect for cracked lips, to other products from other favorite companies. Although, she had to admit, the majority of the items in her bag bore the lavender and cream colors.

"What kind of emergency is this?" he asked, handing Zoe the bag.

"The worst kind any teenager could face," Lexi said

gravely, as she pushed the front door open more. Cool air from inside brushed their faces.

"A pimple," Zoe explained to Will. His brows came together. "Trust me. For a girl about to take photographs that are going to last a lifetime, the last thing she wants is to have a blemish."

"It's not a blemish," Kimber cried from behind the locked bathroom door in the hallway. "It is a new life form."

Zoe tried not to smile as everyone's heels clicked on the hardwood floors. Lexi rapped the back of her hand against the closed door of the bathroom. As Kimber began to tick off her list of demands, which included none of her uncles being present, no cameras and no boys, Zoe tried not to laugh. She remembered these days.

"How bad can it be?" Will tugged on the back of Zoe's shirt and whispered in her ear.

"It's so bad it can hear you," Kimber said from between gritted teeth through the door. "Don't let him in here."

Lexi stepped between Zoe and Will. She took Will by the arm and led him off through the arched doorway. "He's going to sit with Uncle Stephen, sweetie."

"Don't let Uncle Stephen give him a shotgun."

"Gun?" Will repeated, casting a glance back at Zoe. Zoe grinned and shook her head.

"You'll be fine," Lexi told him. "As a matter of fact, I am leaving you in charge."

Zoe didn't see who was seated in the living room but she heard the boom of welcoming male voices and knew Will was in good hands. Lexi walked back down the hallway with a smirk on her face.

"Something more going on between you and the CEO?" Lexi asked. She narrowed her dark eyes at Zoe and folded her arms across her chest. "Did you forget the end game?"

"Of course not," Zoe said. Heat crept up her neck.

"The end game is you as Creative Design Director."

Before having to face Lexi's motherly attitude, Zoe turned to face the door and knocked. "Hey, Kimber, we're alone."

"Are you going to at least answer Aunt Lexi's question first?" Kimber's meek voice asked from the other side.

"Really, Kimber?" Zoe laughed.

"Inquiring minds want to know," Lexi said. She leaned against the wall.

"It would at least make this horrible day better," added Kimber.

Realizing she wasn't going to get anything done, Zoe sighed. "We're getting to know each other."

Is that what she would call it? Had they not been interrupted earlier, Zoe might have let things go a lot further. This afternoon it had been like his hands knew exactly where to go and when. His mouth was magical.

Lexi reached out with her cool hand and pinched Zoe's cheek. "You're turning beet red."

"Ohhh," Kimber sang. "Did you two kiss? He's totally hot."

"Girl, you were wailing three minutes ago about a pimple." Lexi rapped on the door. "Which is more important?"

The doorknob twisted open and the hinges squeaked. "Okay, fine."

"You started that," Zoe whispered before heading inside.

Twenty minutes later, Zoe, Lexi and Kimber emerged from the bathroom with the proper amount of foundation covering her blemish for her pre-prom photo shoot. Zoe promised to come over Saturday afternoon before prom and do Kimber's makeup before attending Lexi's dinner finale for the pageant workers. As a huge favor to Kimber, Zoe did a drastic wingtip over her lid, simply because it would show up better on film. Kimber's prom dress was a Lexi original, made up of bright yellows, oranges and peach. The colors complemented the girl's hazel eyes and golden tan. The prom might be tomorrow night, and there was no telling if Kimber had the votes to become Miss Southwood High's prom queen, but Lexi had plenty of tiaras to choose from.

They found the men in the living room. By "the men," Zoe meant she found Will, Stephen, Nate and a handsome young man dressed in a black tuxedo pinned against the wall by sheer fear. Nate, Stephen's brother, was cleaning what appeared to be a shotgun while Stephen polished his pistol. And Will, not wanting to be left out, sat in a recliner sharpening a bowie knife.

"Seriously?" Kimber wailed. "Aunt Lexi."

With one hand on her hip, Lexi pointed toward the kitchen. "I can't believe you two."

"And you," Zoe added, glaring at Will. "Put that knife down right now. We're about to leave."

"Say goodbye to Will, gentlemen."

Doing as they were told, the brothers rose from their seats. "Bye, Will," they chorused.

Nate Reyes hung his head low so he couldn't flirt

with his green eyes. Last fall Nate had met the love of his life, Amelia Marlow, when she bought him for a hefty fee at the Back to School Bachelor Auction. The "tea," or gossip on the street, was that the two shared a sexy one-night stand and then more. Whatever the truth, Amelia stayed in Southwood and Nate ceased his womanizing ways. Nate patted Zoe's arm on his way into the kitchen. The doorbell rang.

"Luke is going to be here any minute to take you guys for your photo shoot."

"And chaperone!" Stephen called out from the kitchen.

"That's right," both Will and Nate said from either side of the house.

This felt like a glimpse into any future family she might have with Will. He'd be the perfect, overly protective father to their daughter and coach to their son. *Damn it*, Zoe muttered to herself.

Beside her, Lexi cocked her head to the side. "You okay?"

"Oh, yeah." Zoe blinked and brought herself to the present. "I'm fine."

The afternoon sun spilled into the foyer at the front door. Luke stepped inside, hugged both ladies and then performed a man ritual—a handshake and half hug with Will. A few days ago they hadn't known each other. *So?* a voice in Zoe's head taunted her. A few days ago she hadn't known Will either, and now here she was, mentally planning their future.

Outside, the little pink militia saluted them once again. Will led Zoe back to the car with his hand on the small of her back and opened her door. She slid inside and unlocked his.

"That was fun," Will said with a genuine smile. The engine roared to life, just as her heart had from his constant flirting.

"Scaring a teenage boy?"

"I was helping my brethren."

"Brethren?" Zoe laughed, "Boy, you are crazy."

"Stick with me. I'll show you crazy."

Had Will not witnessed what a hurry Zoe was in to get over to Lexi and Stephen's, he would have thought forgetting her hotel key in her childhood bedroom was just a ruse to get him alone again. But since Zoe declined the offer to get to her room through his, he believed her. They arrived back at her family's old home just after dark. There were no cars in the driveway, but that didn't mean Frank Baldwin wasn't outside watching. Even though Frank wanted to encourage a relationship between Will and Zoe, Will did not want an audience. Also not wanting to be tempted to a second session in Zoe's bedroom, Will waited on the hood of the car for Zoe to return from getting her key.

Before the door to the back porch opened with a rickety creak, a light flashed on and then off. "Can you believe my key was on my bed?" Zoe asked moments later as she bounced toward him in the moon's light.

"I can believe you were preoccupied." Will straightened and opened his arms. Zoe instinctively walked into his embrace. "I'm sorry about earlier."

"What's there to be sorry about?" Zoe glanced upward.

To meet her at eye level, Will leaned against the car again. "I don't want the first time anything intimate happens between us to happen on your bed in your childhood home."

"I have to apologize about your family tree." Zoe sighed. "I was pretty obsessed when I was younger. I'm not sure why my dad put them up. I used to have cut out magazines of faces I remade using crayons and markers. Maybe those were too creepy to keep on the walls."

"Yeah," Will teased, "that doesn't sound scary." Whatever the reasons were for the old biographical report pinned on the wall, Will was glad. He was flattered. Zoe impressed him with her attention to detail, and he appreciated her dedication to Ravens Cosmetics.

"Whatever." Zoe pushed his chest. "I am an artist. Anyways, aren't you forward, thinking I was going to let anything go further?"

The key word rolled off her tongue. "Let?" Will repeated.

"Will," Zoe said, "I live a very fast-paced life, but there are some things I like to take my time with. Getting to know someone before sleeping with them is one of them."

It was on the tip of his tongue to mock her with the sleeping part, but she caught on to him and shushed him with her index finger. Will cupped her hand and stroked her finger. "I've got all the time in the world for you, Zoe. As a matter of fact, I think it would be good for us to take things slow."

A light behind the house twinkled in the air. His attention drifted for a moment.

"Because of the job?"

Focusing on her words, Will nodded. "Especially because of the job. I need to know that I'm thinking about the future of my family's company and what the right path to take is." Before Zoe could argue back, Will took his free hand and pressed it against her lips. "I don't want you to be misled about anything."

"You know what's strange?" Zoe began before he had the chance to shush her. "For the first time in my life, Will, I'm not actually thinking about work."

Zoe parted her lips. Under the moonlight he watched breathlessly as her tongue darted along his fingertip. He found his breath again when she pulled it into her mouth and sucked slightly, drawing desire from his body.

"What's on your mind, then?" Will asked, already knowing the answer. She wasn't alone in this. He wanted her. He needed her.

"You," Zoe said, resuming her position against his body. The palm of her hand rested over his heart and its fast beat greeted her. A half grin spread across her face as she looked up with her head turned slightly. Zoe pressed her hand against her own heart. Through the fabric of her T-shirt, her heartbeat fluttered.

An owl hooted and cheered him on as Will lowered his head to brush his lips across Zoe's. There was that familiar sweet taste he'd had before. They fit perfectly together, her cradled against his frame. Will deepened their kiss, his arms wrapped tightly around her waist. He could take her right here and now at the edge of the forest.

"Zoe," Will said, hating to break the kiss. "We need to stop."

"Because of my dad?" Zoe cast a glance over her shoulder, shrugged and looked back up at him. Her long lashes batted against her cheeks. "He's not even home."

"Our first time is not going to be outside."

A wrinkle appeared between her nose and brows. "There you go, thinking I'm going to do something wild with you like that. I'm not that fast."

"Fast, huh?" Will tugged on her hands.

"You know what I mean."

Even with the darkness surrounding them Will could see her cheeks redden. "I already told you, nothing more is happening between us, at least not until we get back home."

"You're so sure of yourself?" Zoe asked. Zoe pressed her hands against his chest and caressed downward across his abs to the waistband of his pants.

Humid evening air filled his lungs. "Zoe," he warned.

The warning went unnoticed. With a defiant raised brow, Zoe locked eyes with him. Her hand slipped beneath his boxers. Just from kissing her, his body went back to his adolescent days and a semi-erection already peaked. When she wrapped her small hands around the base of him, however, he stiffened to granite.

Heat rose between them. Enjoying the sweet torture, Will leaned over and captured her lips with his. Each of her strokes and grip matched the intensity of their tongues. Excitement coursed through his veins. Will broke the kiss and set a thread of kisses along her chin, jaw and neck. With his hands free, Will cupped her breasts, kneading them with his palms. His thumb and forefinger rolled her nipple. Zoe leaned closer. Her hand moved up and down as well as it could within the restriction of his damn pants. Will needed to think. This was not the place he wanted to have a hand job. Blood pounded in his ears. His vision blurred.

"Zoe," Will whispered, "we can't do this here."

Zoe stepped out of Will's embrace. Ice water poured over him. "We're not," she smiled.

Laughing, Will shook his head. "Get in the car, woman, before I change my mind."

Chapter 8

Saturday morning, after tossing and turning all night long, Zoe awoke to the sound of birds chirping outside her window. Still in disbelief of her bold actions last night, Zoe rubbed her eyes with the palm of her hands. It was safe to say there was no turning back now regarding her relationship with Will. Lines were crossed. Zoe's fingers moved from her eyes to her mouth, where her lips tingled from heated dreams of Will. Her heart raced at the thought of seeing him again. Her body shivered with the idea of seeing him alone on the alleged date he said he wanted to take her on when they returned. She couldn't wait.

Eager to see him again, Zoe kicked her comforter off her body and headed for the bathroom. She gave her side of the door a soft knock, just to be safe. No one answered. Not sure why she was disappointed,

Zoe went ahead and took her shower. Steam hung in the air and coated the mirror by the time she finished. A thick, daffodil-yellow towel soaked up the moisture on her body. She tucked it under her arms and wiped down the mirror with her bare hands.

Tonight was their last night at Magnolia Palace. Kenzie had set up a fancy dinner. Yesterday while in the bathroom fixing Kimber's emergency, Lexi had mentioned she planned on sending over a proper dress for tonight's event. Zoe trusted Lexi's taste and couldn't wait to see what her friend chose. She couldn't wait to see Will in his suit. Hell, she couldn't wait to see *him* this morning.

"Hey, Zoe," Will said, knocking on his side of the bathroom door.

Zoe, careful to tiptoe on the rugs to avoid the cold floor on her bare feet, stepped over and opened the door. What did he call her last night? A tease? She'd show him. "Good morning," she said lightly.

From the way he was dressed, in a pair of black baller shorts and a black sleeveless T-shirt, along with the sweat glazing his hard muscles, Will had already been up and working out. He held a piece of perfectly crisp bacon in his big hands.

The look of shock on his face was perfect. Will's mouth dropped open. His eyes immediately went to the droplets of water dribbling from the wet curls of her hair and to the cleavage created by the way she held the towel. The Adam's apple at his throat visibly bobbed up and down as he tried to find words to say.

"Did you need something?"

"Um," Will began. "You have…"

"I have what?" Zoe shook her hair loose with her free hand.

Will blinked several times.

She reached for the lavender bottle of body cream, courtesy of Ravens Cosmetics. "I love this stuff." Zoe held the bottle for him to read the label. He didn't, so she popped the cap open and squirted the magnolia-scented lotion into one hand. Skillfully, she held the towel tucked under her arm and cocked one leg on the counter for a better angle to smear the product on it. The towel was long enough to cover the important parts.

"Will?" She tried to snap but her moistened fingers lacked the friction.

"Sorry," said Will, finally finding his voice. His eyes glanced up to where steam billowed out into his room. "There's someone here for you."

"Someone or some*thing*?" Zoe asked. "Lexi said she was sending over a dress today."

"Someone," Will repeated. He took a bite of his bacon and closed his eyes for a moment while he chewed. Zoe's stomach began to rumble from hunger for food and the man. "Actually, several people are here for you."

Zoe's brows fused together. "What?"

"Get dressed and meet me downstairs."

Curious, it took Zoe a matter of seconds to find a pair of blue gingham shorts and a matching plain blue top. She bounced down the steps toward the sound of chatter. Lots of chatter. The moment her foot hit the bottom step, a gaggle of girls began screaming. Zoe glanced over her shoulder for the rock star who must have been behind her. There was no one. They must have been screaming for her.

"What's going on?" Zoe asked, taking a step back from the wave of practically every flowery and fruity scent possible from Bath & Body Works.

Kenzie made her way through the crowd. "The prom for Southwood High is tonight."

"Yeah, I know."

Some of the girls began wringing their hands together and bobbing at the knees. No one wore a bit of makeup. Zoe looked at all their faces like blank canvases. A twinge jolted through her fingertips as she put two and two together. "Do you guys want some help?"

"Please?" the girls all chorused.

"Did we have plans today?" Zoe asked Kenzie.

"We just have the dinner this evening."

Zoe bit the corner of her lip. She would have loved to hang out with Will today, but this was what she considered an emergency. "Alright, let's form a line. Do any of you have pictures of your gowns with you?" Everyone held their cell phones in the air. The room lit up with colorful glowing screens. "Well then, let's get started. Who was here first?"

The girls all began to speak at once, trying to figure out who was at the head of the line. Other pageant staff was trying to maneuver through the foyer. Even though Zoe didn't use the private elevator, there was another guest who did. Kathleen wheeled out and was blocked by a few of the girls. Rebecca walked out of the dining room and accidently stepped on the toes poking out from one girl's flip-flops. This was not going to work.

Reading her mind, Will sprang into action. "Okay, okay, ladies, let's assemble a line here."

"I was here first."

"No, I was," someone else cried.

There was an easy way to handle this. Zoe stepped up another stair and cupped her hands against her mouth. "Alright, if you're wearing a tube top or something easy to slip over your head, step forward."

Understanding what she was trying to do, Kenzie nodded. "Okay, if you don't have an easy top on, run back home and change into something to slip on. If you need to slip your dress over your head, come back around three." Kenzie turned to glance up at Zoe for approval. She nodded. "Okay, let's get to it."

"I don't understand what's going on," Will whispered.

She didn't expect him to. Zoe patted the center of his back. "Those girls are going to put on their dresses over their heads, so the last thing they're going to want to do is smear their makeup on the material of the gown."

"I can help." Rebecca moved toward the stairs and held on to the banister. "I can do hair."

"And I can do nails," said a pageant staffer, Lily Ortiz, from the banister at the top of the stairs. The pretty nail tech and Zoe worked together in the past at fashion expos.

"Sounds like everyone has a job," Zoe said. "Alright, let's get to it."

All the girls began to scatter. Some began forming a single-file line while others trotted out the front door. Zoe turned and found Will staring at her with awe. He stood a step above her, causing her to stare right at his chest. The muscle shirt he wore revealed the work he put in at the gym. A long vein bulged down each bicep.

Will tipped her chin toward him with a brush of his finger. "What do you need me to do?"

"Probably nothing," Zoe said honestly.

A crash came from around the corner. Some of the men from the bed-and-breakfast rushed to the rescue. Luke backed out of the room carrying a broken vase. Ramon pushed his door open and accidentally hit another girl in the back of her legs.

"I've got an idea," said Will. "How about we start an assembly line of sorts in my room? The girls can hang out in there and come through our bathroom to keep out of the way down here."

Zoe sighed with appreciation. "You wouldn't mind?"

"Not all," Will said, sliding his hands into the pockets of his shorts. "I was still at home when my sisters started dating. Our house was pure chaos."

"This isn't just a date," Zoe reminded him. They started walking up the stairs together. The girls waddled in their heels behind them like ducks. "This is the prom."

"Well, if you remember, I wasn't home for prom."

"I didn't have a prom either," Zoe said, elbowing him in the ribs, "but I at least can remember how much I wanted to get all dressed up and go."

"Ah," Will began to counter, sliding his forefinger against the slope of her nose. Her cheeks flushed with heat at the touch. "You went to Comic-Con, though."

Zoe hid the sly smile by turning her head to the side. "Dressing up as the ultimate warrior princess was worth missing my prom."

Will placed both hands on her shoulders. She glanced up into his dark eyes and a flutter rushed in the pit of her stomach. "Wait, you dressed up in a frayed leather skirt and bustier?"

Her response was a grin. She already saw the wheels in his head turning. No, she didn't still have the outfit, but Zoe did have a pair of black spikey boots and star-spangled panties. Didn't everyone?

"You two should totally come tonight," blurted out one of the girls closest to the two of them. "I'm on the prom committee and I could totally get you in. You guys would totally be the coolest chaperones."

Will paused at the top step for a moment and wiggled his brows. "I'm totally up for the after-prom," he whispered in Zoe's ear. Some of the girls giggled. Maybe not at what he said, but at the way Zoe stumbled on the step.

Later on in the afternoon, after a trip to the ice cream shop for milk shakes and the pizza parlor for pizza and wings, Will returned to the hotel. The cars had disappeared from the parking lot. The lines had thinned down to a few girls getting their hair and nails done in the dining room and living room. He wondered if Zoe was finished. Will thought of the Creative Design Director position. Zoe displayed great leadership when it came to organizing the girls. She didn't panic, and her generosity in sharing her skills with these girls in their time of need humbled him. He wasn't sure how many of the interviewees would have taken time out of their day to help.

Because he'd been running back and forth all afternoon, he never got a chance to see the prom girls when Zoe was done with them. Will hated to admit he was frightened at first to see what kind of looks she'd placed on the girls. This would have been a live résumé for her. All the jobs in her portfolio were of heavily made-up people, although there were several artistic pictures. But Ravens Cosmetics didn't need artwork displayed on its clients' faces.

What Will wouldn't mind seeing, however, was a repeat of the view from this morning when she'd opened the door after her shower. The droplets of water against her brown skin haunted his brain, in a pleasant way. Damn, he couldn't take much more of this torture.

"Oh, hey, there you are." Kenzie's voice caught Will's attention. She rounded the corner from the kitchen with a pile of black garment bags in her arms blocking her face.

Will hurried toward her. "Let me get those. What are you doing with all of this stuff?"

"Evening attire," said Kenzie. She stretched her arms, then massaged her biceps. "Courtesy of Grits and Glam Gowns."

Lexi's shop, Will remembered. He draped the bags over one arm. "Where do you want the rest of these?"

"Come with me," Kenzie said, waving her arm down the other hallway. "We start down here."

As they made their way to each female guest's door, Kenzie went on about how excited she was about tonight. Even Will started to get excited. With each delivery of a dress, the ladies all squealed with youthful excitement, much like the teenagers from this morning.

"Have you enjoyed your time here at Magnolia Palace?" Kenzie asked. They waited for the elevator. She insisted he not climb the stairs with the rest of the garments.

Will nodded. "This place has been wonderful."

"I'm kind of partial to it, myself."

"Are you and Ramon partners?"

"No!" Kenzie hissed. Her light brown cheeks reddened and her lips pressed together. Quickly she shook her head and tucked a stray hair behind her ear. "I mean, we're not partners. I just have a deep-rooted attachment to this place."

"Did your parents get engaged here, like Zoe's folks?"

"Yes, but that's not the only reason." Kenzie regained herself. "This house used to belong to my family, back before the turn of the twentieth century."

"No kidding?"

"Never would kid," said Kenzie. "But during hard times, the structure was lost by the original builders and turned over to family members who made more bad investments in wartime."

"Until Ramon Torres came along?" Will asked. The elevator arrived at the second floor. Will waved his free hand for Kenzie to exit.

"Yes," Kenzie answered, looking at him over her shoulder.

Will nodded. "Smart of him to listen to you."

"Smart of me to be the town historian."

"That's a real thing, huh?" Will asked.

"Of course." Kenzie's cell phone rang. She glanced at the caller ID and declined the call. Will wondered if the *R* he saw pop up on her screen stood for Ramon. "Enough about my family drama. I can take the rest of the dresses down the hall if you'll give this one to Zoe."

At the sound of her name, Will grew excited. The pit of his stomach shifted with an odd feeling. "I can do that," he said coolly.

"Thanks, and I'll see you later tonight."

Will headed toward his room first. He wanted to clean himself up before seeing Zoe again. Since his door was closed, he assumed the girls had disappeared. He opened the door and the smell of flowers was now faint.

"I don't want to look like all the other girls," said a young voice.

"You're not," Zoe said to whomever was in her room. "I made sure no one was exactly the same."

"Except for your signature wingtip."

Zoe's light chuckle filled the air. Will smiled as he eavesdropped. This week he'd figured out what a wingtip was and saw how Zoe *perfected* it, as she liked to boast.

"But I want to look like Lil' Get This. Your Instagram with her got the most likes I've ever seen."

Lil' Get This, Will recalled with a sneer, who'd posed basically naked on her CD cover. The only thing the young rap artist had worn was Zoe's makeup. The photo was absent from Zoe's portfolio, but that didn't mean Will hadn't seen it.

"Lil' Get This is a professional artist."

Will would use that term loosely.

"You're going to have to remember that those ladies you see on my Instagram are going for a particular look, which is why they look that way," Zoe explained. "You don't think they walk around with a full face of makeup all day, do you?"

"Yeah, well, maybe. I've seen what you did with the teen girls on BET's Black Girls Rock show."

"I see you follow my work."

"I used to collect all the different magazines your models were in, but my mom said she'd kill me if I brought in any more clutter." The girl's statement reminded Will of what Zoe's parents might have said to her. Didn't she say she used to apply beauty products to the already printed magazine pages?

"So I have a page on my blog dedicated to your work." The girl continued naming all of Zoe's accomplishments. "I love the eighties, thanks to you. Music videos were the best."

"That's so sweet," Zoe sighed.

Will imagined Zoe beaming with pride at this moment. He pictured her cheeks turning red or her biting her bottom lip and avoiding a gaze.

"You're really cool. But I still want to look like someone else. I want to look like a star."

"Lisa," Zoe said, "you don't need all that heavy makeup to make you look like a star. Think of all the faces I've done. They're like superheroes. And like all superheroes, they are wearing a mask, but when they are just being themselves, they don't need all that extra stuff to hide their beauty. Does that make sense?"

"No." The word came out more with a whine but accompanied by a laugh. "But okay."

"When you get old enough, you can put your makeup on however you like, but for now, just enjoy being a kid and enjoy your prom."

"Thanks, Miss Zoe."

When Will heard Zoe's door close, he crossed through their bathroom and leaned against the door. From this angle it appeared her bottom half was encased in a pair of tube socks with three pink stripes. Zoe wore an apron with I Love Makeup spelled out in makeup items, such as a tube of mascara for the *I*, two eyeliner pencils making the *L*, red lipstick spelling

out the *O* in a heart shape, and a powder brush as the
E. The word *makeup* was spelled out in eyeliner. Her
pink apron held several pockets, each containing either
a variety of lipsticks, an eyelash contraption he'd seen
his sisters use, or powder brushes. Zoe's long brown
hair was piled up in a loose bun. Several strands had
come loose from the band securing her tresses. Different shades of powder sprinkled her face. The insides of
her forearms were streaked with various pink, mauve,
red, gold and brown shades. She'd never looked more
beautiful.

"Long day?" Will asked. He expected Zoe to fret
about her hair or her attire. But, instead, she straightened her shoulders and stood tall.

"Yes, but I had a blast."

Will crossed the room, the garment bag under his
arm. "I have something for you."

It was his intent to hand her the dress, but when she
opened her arms, who was he to resist? Will set the
bag on the edge of her bed and pulled Zoe's body into
his. Their mouths met for two or three polite kisses,
just lips, but then they fed into their desire, tongues
circling fiercely together. His hands dragged across her
bottom, fitting underneath the cuffs of her blue-and-
white shorts. The ties of her apron brushed against the
backs of his hands.

"I could get used to a greeting like that every day,"
Will breathed, breaking the kiss and brushing the tip
of his nose against hers.

"Tell me about it." Zoe stroked the side of his face.
He turned his face to kiss her palm. They needed to
stop.

Though he shouldn't, Will thought of being able to

kiss Zoe like this every day. Every day at the office or every day at home. If she became the Creative Design Director, he wouldn't be able to do this. There'd have to be some boundaries, and right now, Will didn't want to test those.

Zoe stepped backward with her hands on her hips. "I need to start cleaning up in here before dinner tonight."

"Speaking of dinner," Will said, remembering the garment bag. "Kenzie delivered these for you from Lexi's." Like the other ladies had at their doors, Zoe squealed with excitement. Her face lit up as she yanked down the bag's zipper. Before Will had a chance to see, Zoe pressed the dress against her chest. "What?"

"Isn't it bad luck to see the dress?" Zoe wiggled her eyebrows at him.

"I believe that's for a wedding. We haven't had our first official date," Will replied and gave a lopsided grin. "We can start things off tonight, though. Care to be my date for the dinner?"

For a moment, Zoe glanced at the ceiling and pondered his question. "It is rather late to be asking."

"Someone's already asked?" Will faked being upset—or, rather, covered the bubble in his gut. He turned toward the door. "Who had the nerve to ask after I've staked my claim to you this week?"

"Staked," Zoe laughed, grabbing Will back by the arm. "What am I? An uncharted territory?"

He liked the way her hand fit around his biceps—made it totally worth working out all the time. Will caught her hand and pulled her up to him once again. Without thinking he lowered his head and his lips to hers. "I can't wait to explore."

Chapter 9

In the end, Zoe, of course, gave in to Will's request and allowed him to take her to dinner. It didn't hurt that he knocked on her door carrying a bouquet of flowers or that he became utterly speechless at the sight of her when she let him in.

She had to hand it to Lexi and her choice of dress. The floor-length black evening gown was flawless. A diamond band cinched her waistline and the strapless sweetheart neckline helped accentuate her assets. She wished she'd thought to bring her grandmother's good-luck pearls for this evening, but settled for a pair of diamond teardrop earrings instead. For dramatic effect, Lexi had sent along a pair of black evening gloves. Thankfully, tugging the hem of the gloves over her elbows distracted her from converting into a cartoon character with her eyes popping out of her head and her jaw dropping to the floor at Will, who was amazingly handsome in his crisp black tuxedo.

What took her breath away was the way the covered area out back at Mas was set up. Someone had taken it upon themselves to put lights on the ceiling, making it seem like they were dining under the stars. Kenzie had tuxedoed waiters to serve their meals. A long, triangular table held everyone working on the pageant and was covered with white linen cloths; someone had had the foresight to bring in free-standing air conditioners and place them at each corner. Some of the tables had been taken out and in their place was a portable dance floor. Soft music pumped into the area.

Dinner was a combination of Southern battered chicken and catfish, green beans with ham, and macaroni and cheese. Sweet tea filled the glasses and laugher echoed in the air.

"I can't believe I've had such a great week," Will said, covering Zoe's left gloved hand. They were seated together, and it wasn't the first time Zoe had felt the jitters each time he accidentally brushed against her leg or her arm.

Zoe bumped her shoulder against his arm. "Are the pressures of being CEO off?"

"Not off, just on hold."

"But after tomorrow you'll be back to the grind."

Will gave her hand a squeeze. "But now I've got you in my life."

Again the butterflies returned. She couldn't wait to spend time with Will at home, walk on the beach and dine across a moonlit table—just the two of them.

"I'm sorry to break up this lovefest," Kenzie said.

"Sure you are," Ramon mumbled, loud enough for

a few people around to hear when the music was lowered via remote control.

Judging from the way Kenzie rolled her eyes, she heard it, too. She rose from her seat at the head of the table and clinked her glass with her spoon. She continued until she reached the center of the dance floor where someone mysteriously had placed a podium. "Our host, Lexi Pendergrass Reyes, couldn't be here this evening, but she wanted the night to continue."

A round of applause broke out. Zoe wondered if Lexi's absence meant Stephen had made her stay home because tomorrow was going to be a big day or because the baby was ready to make an appearance two months early. Surely Zoe would have received a text message or something.

"This week we all got the chance to get to know each other," Kenzie began. "We've seen the hard work put into making a pageant by the lighting people, stage hands, artists and even the judges." Kenzie glanced at everyone who made up part of the crew. "Hopefully we've bonded enough to trust each other's opinions come tomorrow. Whether it's with the makeup and hair, or when it comes to the judging."

Another round of applause.

Zoe glanced around at the people she'd gotten to know this week and figured everyone had some common sense. Even Rebecca had come around and performed selflessly that morning. She half expected the hairstylist to not give the prom girls the time of day. The only person Zoe thought might cause problems was the beauty queen, Vera Laing. According to Lexi, she'd invited Vera, her former student, to judge but worried their relationship had suffered irrevocable damage. Lexi trained the beauty queen from the time she was a toddler but left because of a conflict of interest. Lexi loved Vera but never knew what Vera had been told about the circumstances of Lexi's departure. Vera and her mother were the only two who had not wanted to participate in any of the activities. This was simply a free vacation for them.

"So, in order to commemorate our time together, Ramon and I have been gathering intel and we've put a lot of thought and consideration together last night to come up with a list of awards we want to hand out to you all."

Ramon stood and walked to the podium with a rolled-up piece of paper in his hands. Zoe got the feeling he didn't want to do this, but she knew how persuasive Kenzie could be. It was the first time Zoe had seen Ramon in a suit and he looked rather handsome. His black hair was slicked back and off his face, and finally Zoe saw the resemblance between him and his cousins Stephen and Nate.

"First and foremost, thanks for coming to my hotel," Ramon said, leaning into the microphone. "This has been a successful week and it's been a pleasure getting to know you."

Beside him, Kenzie cleared her throat.

"Ah, yes, we gave this a lot of thought and consideration last night."

Last night? Zoe thought with bewilderment. *Hmm, what's going on here?* She certainly knew what she'd been doing last night. Zoe placed her hand in Will's lap and squeezed his leg. His eyes darted to her. Zoe stared straight ahead and began drawing circles on his pants leg up his thigh. The bulge between his legs grew and pressed against her arm.

"…and so for the most helpful one, especially since he helped me fix all these lights up here," Ramon was saying, "I'd like to present the award of Most Handy to Tim Hernandez."

The crowd clapped again, and to Zoe's surprise, Kenzie reached under the podium and presented Tim with a gold statue.

Awards were given out left and right. Most Helpful, Most Spirit, Most Southern. Zoe entertained herself with fondling Will. She enjoyed the way he inhaled each time she cupped his crotch through his pants. His erection grew, turning her on even more. She stroked, squeezed and turned herself on with the image of herself riding him. Will's jaw twitched.

"And for the…" Ramon stopped and turned toward Kenzie. His hand covered the microphone but his muffled words were heard. "Do I really have to say it?"

"It's not going to kill you," Kenzie huffed.

Will reached for Zoe's hand and put it back on the table, wagging his index finger. He leaned so close to her ear his breath tickled her lobe. "Be careful what you start, my little tease."

"Whatever." Zoe pressed her lips together to keep from grinning.

"Whatever," Ramon said into the microphone. "We conclude this awards ceremony with the—" he cleared his throat "—with the cutest couple." He said the words as if they pained him. "Will Ravens and Zoe Baldwin."

Shocked, Zoe shook her head. "Oh, we're not…"

"Not fooling anyone," Kenzie said, pushing Ramon

away from the microphone. "Now, come on up here and get this award."

Zoe didn't get a chance to protest. After buttoning his jacket as he rose and hunched over, Will extended his hand for Zoe to take and positioned her in front of him. She obliged, knowing what she hid for him from the rest of the guests. The table clapped for them as they made their way to the podium. Ramon handed Will an envelope and Kenzie handed Zoe a gold statue of two silhouettes kissing.

"Now, let's conclude this evening with a dance."

Will took Zoe by the hand and led her to the floor. She stood against him, fitting perfectly. She took his hand and the music began, though she barely heard the melody. Others began to crowd the dance floor.

"Well, you have to admit," Will said, "we are the cutest couple."

"We are the *only* couple."

"Are we?" Will inclined his head toward Kenzie and Ramon. The two were dancing closely together, but the tight grin across Kenzie's face said something else.

Zoe turned her attention back to Will. Her heart fluttered. There was something Zoe was supposed to do or say to stop him from kissing her in front of everyone, but she couldn't think of what it was. Their bodies began to fall into perfect rhythm.

"This can't be good," Will whispered against her neck.

If things didn't cool off, Zoe was about to melt in his arms. Her eyes rolled backward with the warmth of his breath. "If it ain't good..." she began.

"Zoe, I need you," Will said, licking his lips.

The only thing Zoe heard was he needed her—that,

and her Prince ringtone going off inside the pocket of her clutch bag. Will pressed his head against her forehead. "Go ahead and answer that."

Will pressed his hands on her backside and guided Zoe back to their table where she retrieved her cell phone. She attempted to slide her finger across the screen but her gloves gave her a bit of a fit. She slipped them off her arms and swiped her finger across Lexi's face.

"Hey, girl," Zoe said, trying to sound cheerful, pushing off the feeling that a bucket of ice had doused her evening. Thank God for the portable air conditioners. Zoe glided toward one and let it cool off her body. "Are you okay?"

"I'm fine," Lexi said. "I am watching a live feed from bed."

"What?" Zoe held her phone by her side and glanced around until she spotted a red light mixed in with the faux stars. "What are you doing?"

"Saving your potential career," Lexi said. "I saw you and Will just now."

"So?"

"When I saw y'all's name on the list for cutest couple, I thought it was a joke. Jesus, Zoe, you're applying for a position in his company."

The proverbial cold water continued to fall, dousing any inkling of a hot night. "Okay, Lexi. I understand."

After a few more lines about not messing up and sleeping where you work, Lexi had drilled the message into Zoe's head. Like a child having been scolded, Zoe hung up the phone and crossed her arms over her chest.

"Is everything okay?" Will asked the question as his hands warmed her shoulders. She hadn't realized the AC had chilled her to her bones. Or maybe it was Lexi's words. Either way, Zoe stepped out of Will's embrace and turned to face him.

"I'm fine." Zoe half smiled. An ache squeezed her heart. Common sense told her she'd find someone else, sooner or later. Right now her priority was landing the Creative Design Director job with Ravens Cosmetics. "You know, it's been a long day. I probably need to head on back to the hotel and rest up for tomorrow."

Nodding, Will reached for her again, successfully pressing his hand against her lower back. "Let me tell everyone we're leaving."

"No," Zoe exclaimed, holding her hand in the air. "The last thing I need is for everyone to see us leaving together."

"I'm sorry." Will shoved his hands in his front pockets and cocked his head as if it gave him a better understanding of what she said. "Did I miss something?"

"No."

"We were having a good time just a few minutes ago." He reached for her again and in order to not make a scene, Zoe let him.

The brush against her arm sent chills down her spine. In the few seconds she tried to keep him away, his touch created such a sensation throughout her body she realized that she needed it. Zoe blinked toward the lights overhead to keep from letting a teardrop fall. She needed to focus. "We were having a good time, Will. But I need a break. I've got to go."

Foolishly, Zoe had left with no secured plan on how to get back to the hotel. She headed down Mas's driveway toward the street. In her dress and heels, she regretted her decision to leave the party. Zoe slid her phone open, searched for an Uber driver near her and placed an order for a pickup.

Less than five minutes later a car pulled up to the mailbox. But it wasn't the Uber car she'd called. Instead, it was a stretch limousine. The back window rolled down and a gaggle of girls screamed Zoe's name. In the center of the group of girls sticking out of the sunroof was Kimber Reyes, toting a crown so big it caught the moonlight across the crystals.

"Evening, ladies," Zoe said, cheering up. When she'd last checked her phone the time was close to midnight. Didn't they have curfews? "What are you doing out this late?"

"After-party!" someone yelled.

"We wanted to sneak and get a look at your party," Kimber said.

"Like, you saved all of us today," another girl said.

Someone popped the door open and Zoe sighed as she climbed in. "Well, thanks for the lift. How was the prom?"

Everyone began to talk at once. The space of the limo was filled with girls and Zoe wondered where all their dates were, but someone else mentioned again about an after-party about to get started. The story the girls gave was that they'd all been together since elementary school and they started out every party together. They'd promised each other that once they were seniors, no matter what cliques they were in, they'd all hang out together at prom. They'd managed to do the same thing for every party throughout middle and high school. Zoe liked the idea of the girls all sticking together rather than focusing on being with boys.

It was the confirmation Zoe needed to stay focused on her goals.

The limousine made its way to the front steps of Magnolia Palace. "Are you guys coming to the pageant tomorrow?" Zoe asked with her hand on the door before their chauffeur could open it.

"I'll be there all day," Kimber said with a droll roll of her eyes. "Come hell or high water, I've got to be there."

"Why the long face?" Zoe asked.

"Because y'all are starting at the crack of dawn, which limits how long I can stay out tonight."

Zoe grinned and patted Kimber's shoulder. "Behave tonight."

"I'd say the same to you," Kimber teased right back. "But considering you've gone home alone, I'm guessing you have no choice."

"You're cute."

"And you're pretty," said Kimber. "Don't waste your pretty."

Unprepared for the girl's rather grown-up response, Zoe burst out in laughter. "Get going, child. I'll see you tomorrow."

The girls went on down the road, chanting for the driver to lay on the limo's horn. Zoe headed upstairs, laughing the whole way to her room. She was glad for the peace and quiet.

Not wanting to get out of her gorgeous dress so soon, Zoe kicked off her heels and headed into the bathroom to begin her nightly rituals. A part of her felt guilty for leaving Will at the party without so much as an explanation. As she reached for Ravens Cosmetics's makeup-remover cream, Zoe realized he deserved to know why she left. But if she'd told him, he would only have tried to convince her she was wrong. What she was, was swept up with the Southern heat. After wiping the last remnants of cream off her face, Zoe heard a knock. Her heart slammed against her rib cage.

"I know you're in there," Will said from the other side of the door.

Zoe contemplated tiptoeing back to her room, but she wanted to lay eyes on him before going to bed. If she couldn't have him in real life, she could always dream about him. "Why did you leave the dinner?" Zoe asked, opening the door.

The black bowtie hung loose around Will's neck and the top three buttons of his white shirt were undone. The cut of his shirt complemented his hard jawline.

"I left because finding out what's going on with you is more important than sitting at the table watching everyone else dance."

Zoe shrugged her shoulders. "There were other people you could have danced with."

"I only wanted you." Will reached for her hand, pressing it against his beating heart. "What changed when you took that phone call?"

"What are you talking about?"

"Don't act like I don't know you by now, Zoe."

Zoe took a step backward. "No, what you know is the Zoe who has had her head fogged up in these Southern nights. Not the Zoe you met over a week ago when I applied for the director's position."

"Zoe," Will sighed.

She'd heard what he said about not liking her work. She didn't care. "Until I get an official word on Ravens Cosmetics stationery thanking me for the time but saying y'all have decided to go in a different direction, I still have a fighting chance."

"And so I have no say in this?" Will asked, letting her hand go.

"Not really. Save your say for something official, and then let's go from there. Right now I don't want to risk what I've worked so hard for."

Will's mouth dropped open. He stood in the doorway, gawking. "You're serious."

"As a heart attack."

"And what about your personal life, Zoe?" Will asked. "You want to stand here and say your career is worth more than your happiness?"

Zoe wasn't sure what the answer was. She shrugged her shoulders and stepped backward.

"You want to stand here and tell me what's been brewing between us is just some Southern spell?"

"Yes," Zoe said, finding her voice. "We'll have to wait for everything business between us to be over."

"And if you start with Ravens Cosmetics?" asked Will. "We're supposed to act like there's nothing between us?"

"Looks that way."

"So, either way I'm being punished?"

Zoe narrowed her eyes on his face. His lips were thin and his jawline twitched. It killed her to deny them what they both wanted. Her body trembled with such craving. "Will, you're utterly handsome, heir to the throne of Ravens Cosmetics. You're bothered that you're not getting your own way. And I dare say you're pouting."

"Pouting?" Will snorted out a laugh.

Zoe threw her hands in the air and backed farther away. "Whatever. I'm going to bed."

"And just like that," Will called out to her, "you're done talking?"

"Yep," Zoe yelled over her shoulder, "looks that way to me." She attempted to kick the door to the bathroom closed with the heel of her bare foot and out of the corner of her eye saw a lightning-like bolt darting toward her.

"Good, because I'm done talking, too."

Will came up behind Zoe and wrapped his arms around her waist. She had just enough time to spin around, face him and open her mouth to protest. Will braced her backside and dipped her. His mouth descended on hers and Zoe loved every moment of it. Will's left hand slid down the length of her dress and lowered the zipper, exposing her to his touch. His fingers were like feathers, tickling and caressing every inch of her. Zoe's right leg curled up and wrapped around his waist. She moaned against him.

Not breaking the kiss, Will lifted Zoe in his arms and brought her over to her bed. The soft mattress absorbed their weight. Will's magical mouth made love to hers. His hands played with skin, toyed with her nipples and rolled one between his thumb and forefinger. Juices of flat-out desire flowed through her veins.

"W—" Zoe tried to say his name when he broke the kiss, but when she pulled her head back he pressed his finger against her lips. She waited with anticipation as he moved down her body. He left a trail of sensual kisses behind her ear, neck and throat, and between her breasts. Her nipples throbbed in anticipation of the warmth of his mouth. She closed her eyes tight as she grew dizzy. Humidity hung in the air, but when Will's tongue circled her nipples, she realized how cool her flesh was. She hadn't known just how much she needed him.

Will set another trail of kisses down the curve of her belly. Warm air filtered through her black panties, and when his fingers breached the material Zoe's hips bucked forward. Zoe discovered he had at some point moved his finger from her mouth when he used both hands to slide her panties over her hips. Using his thumbs, he gently caressed the tender skin of her upper thigh. Zoe opened her legs wider for him to touch. She throbbed for him.

Will leaned forward, and as Zoe inhaled deeply, he satiated her craving for his touch by delving his tongue into the folds of her lips. Zoe gasped silently and stared upward, where their shadows danced on the ceiling. Heat lightning flashed outside the bay windows. Her toes curled. Will's tongue licked up and down, sucking and devouring. He sank his forefinger into her wet flesh, and she quivered and wantonly moved her legs over his broad shoulders. Each time she moaned, he pressed further with his ministrations. A wave of what Zoe expected to be the first of many orgasms came.

Another bolt of heat lightning flashed against Will's face. He grinned smugly and shrugged out of his shirt. Zoe didn't dare speak. She licked her lips in eagerness and scrambled to her knees. The palms of her hands itched, wanting to touch him again. Will stood, unbuttoned his trousers and shrugged out of them and his briefs at the same time. His arousal was evident, with the massive erection pointing toward her as he rolled a clear condom over it. Zoe reached her hand to take him but he gently pushed her hand away.

"Will?" she cried, her brows fusing together.

"You had your chance to talk, Zoe." Will inched closer to her. "You've told me all the reasons why we shouldn't be together and now I'm going to show you why we need to be together."

In the darkness Will reached for the back of her thigh and, in one swift swoop, landed her flat on her back. In the process, Zoe wrapped her legs around Will's waist. Will's thick shaft pressed into her with ease. They both gasped when he fully filled her. A switch went off between the two of them. Their mouths clicked together and they found their perfect rhythm. Zoe's head swam with dizziness. This was so right. So perfect. She moaned and arched her hips. Will pumped deeper. Even though she was on her back, the sensation of free-falling washed over her. Zoe clung to Will's back, and he rolled over and positioned her on top of him.

With her knees supporting her weight, Zoe rocked back and forth, grinding her body against his. She set the tempo to a ballroom foxtrot—quick, quick, slow. Will groaned and eased himself up so she sat in his lap. He feasted on her breasts and Zoe wrapped her arms around his neck again. Sweat drizzled between their bodies. Will nibbled her chin and licked her collarbone. His hands tightened their grip on her body, skin against skin, and guided the rhythm as he drove into her. Zoe bounced and called out his name. At one point, Zoe tossed her head back in the throes of another spectacular orgasm and noticed the rain coming down outside. Water poured against the glass as Zoe melted onto Will. He crisscrossed his arms across her back and pulled her down by the shoulders, then rolled with her, so her back was against the mattress.

Will covered her mouth with his. Zoe mewed against him. She didn't know where she wanted to touch him next. Her fingers splayed on his chest. Will lifted his head, offered a lopsided grin, then pulled her hands over her head and pushed against the headboard. Balancing himself on his elbows, Will stared into her eyes and made love to her visually and physically. He looked as if he was taking in an art piece. She felt exquisite and desired.

A tear threatened at the corner of her eye. She might have cried if another orgasm hadn't taken over. Will's body sped up and shivered as they climaxed at the same time. Any bit of doubt she may have had over the two of them being together was washed away.

Chapter 10

Like the rain, the power of the storm between Zoe and Will subsided. At the crack of dawn Will rose from his well-earned slumber. Zoe lay on her side facing him. Her hands were folded in a prayer position beneath her cheek. The only thing missing was a halo over her cute, messy bed head. She looked like an angel. Will smiled when her long lashes fluttered against her cheekbones.

Last night had been incredible. His heart filled with something unfamiliar. He never wanted this moment to end. Zoe belonged with him. Somehow he needed to figure things out. Since watching Zoe with the prom girls and hearing her explanation about appropriate makeup, Will's vehemence about her being over-the-top had subsided.

"Young William," a feminine voice called out.

If Will wasn't mistaken, it sounded a lot like his

sister Eva. She was the one who called him that. Will guessed from sound of the knock that she was at his door. This also meant her twin was somewhere close. This was the last thing he needed.

"Let me do it. Jerraud taught me a few tricks with locks."

So Dana was here, as well. Naked, Will slid out of the bed and trotted back through the bathroom. He locked his side for privacy and sanity.

"You and your husband have problems," Eva said.

"What? We have hobbies."

Will grabbed a pair of red ballers and slipped them on before he opened the door. Dana, on her knees, caught her balance before hitting the floor. Eva, however, tripped over her sister.

"Is spying on your brother one of them?" Will asked. He leaned over to help Eva to her feet. Though she was older by a few years, she was still a foot shorter than he was.

"Will," Eva and Dana chorused.

"Eva wanted to see the pageant." Dana brushed her hands together. "I wanted to see Sasha Foxx again. It's been a while since we walked down the runway together."

"Whatever. I came partially for the pageant," Eva said, rolling her eyes. "My other reason is to figure out what's going on between you and Zoe Baldwin."

The mention of her name made his heart jump. Will knew he wanted Zoe to be a part of his life for a while. He just wasn't sure he wanted his family to know yet. Clearly Dana already discussed Zoe with Eva. It was only a matter of time before whatever story

Dana came up with would spread to the family. "She's in her room."

"And you know this how?" asked Eva. She sauntered into the room, her head turning as she snooped in every direction. "Where were you last night?"

"I thought there was a formal dinner," Dana added.

Here came the inquisition. "There was," Will answered.

"Where's your suit?" Eva asked, opening the closet. "It's not on the floor and you never pick up after yourself."

Will trotted to the closet and closed the doors before Eva discovered it missing. "What exactly are you two doing in Southwood?"

"We wanted to watch the pageant," the girls chorused. Their sound came out in sync, with Eva beside him with her hand still jiggling the closet handle and Dana on the other side inspecting his made-up bed.

Damn. Will leaned against the closed closet and watched the twins spy. Thank God he hadn't brought Zoe in here last night. Thinking of her put a smile to his face. To be sure he didn't act on his thought, Will swiped his hand down his face. He needed to shave. Hell, he needed to shower. Along with the long list of things Will needed to do, he needed to figure out what the twins were up to. They glanced nervously back and forth at each other.

"There's more you're not telling me," he said.

"And there's something you're not telling us," Dana said, changing the subject. His sisters were nosy, but this nosy? "Like, who have you been with, Will?"

Avoidance? Will scratched the top of his head. "What's going on with the company?"

"Nothing." Dana shrugged her shoulders. "The whole board came into Southwood."

"What?" Will did a double take. The idea of his cousins, all the cousins, being there did not sit right with him. He got that RC provided the makeup. Did they make a personal trip just to deliver the goods?

"They're just here. No big deal. Don't worry about it." Eva pushed Will by the shoulder. Easy for her to say. Eva stood on her tiptoes and took a whiff of air. As Will dodged one sister by sidestepping her, the other came up behind him and inhaled. "You smell like you've been using our products."

"What's going on, Will?" Dana asked. "Why are you so jumpy?"

"I'm jumpy because you started banging on my door at the crack of dawn," said Will. "Where's the rest of the group? I know y'all don't travel too far without them." He waited a moment to hear the sound of destruction from his nieces and nephews.

"This is a business trip," they said again in unison, and giggled at themselves.

"The anti-cousins were, uh," Eva began, "not too happy when they learned from Marcus that Zoe Baldwin was here as the beauty consultant."

"Great," Will mumbled. "Which ones are here?"

"Dixon, Katie, Brandon and Charles." Eva used her fingers to tick off the names. "And Cora came."

"Cora's neutral," Will said. One of the youngest of the Ravens, Cora was too busy living her life as a college student to helm a corporation.

"She didn't think it was fair that one interviewee got special treatment."

Irritation consumed Will. His knuckles cracked as

he made a fist. This would be worse for Zoe now if she did get the position. Knowing Will and Zoe had spent time here together might bug Cora enough to side with the anti-cousins.

"I don't get why they're so quick to make a decision on the position if they are ready to call it quits. Something doesn't add up."

"Your guess is as good as mine," Dana sighed. "But you know we have your back in whatever decision you make."

"Well, if you ladies don't mind, I need to get dressed."

Dana was the first to roll her eyes. "Whatever. We used to change your diapers when you were little."

Eva punched him in the arm. "Don't be so modest."

"I'm grown now," Will clarified and puffed out his chest. "Let the record show, you two forced me to play house with you when I was walking and out of diapers."

There was a laundry list of things Will wanted to say to prove to his sisters he was a grown man but Dana's phone rang.

"No," Dana sighed. "We're up in his room. No, he's awake."

For a moment Will wondered who his sister was on the phone with, but he heard Donovan's distinct deep voice on the other end of the call. "Get out of his room so he can get ready."

"Fine, whatever," Dana huffed.

The next time he went out with his brother, Will was buying for the night. He strolled over to the bedroom door and yanked it open. "Tell Donovan I owe him."

The girls began to leave, but not before Eva sized him up. "We're not done here, mister."

And somehow Will knew they weren't. Once the

girls left, Will pressed his ear against the door to make sure his nosy sisters' voices traveled down the stairs. The first thing he needed to do was make sure Zoe was okay and, hopefully, still asleep. He pulled open the bathroom door and found Zoe leaning against the double sink with her arms folded. Long, dark strands of hair spilled over her shoulders. A yellow-and-white polka-dot towel was wrapped around her succulent brown body. Jealous of the terrycloth material, Will forgot what he wanted to say.

"So," Zoe sighed with a grin. "You wore diapers longer than the average child, huh?"

"You heard that?" Will bit his bottom lip to keep from cursing and quite possibly blushing over this revealed secret.

"Just the most important part." Zoe giggled. "I bet you were a cute kid. I can't wait to see pictures of you when you were younger. Did they dress you up, too?"

"My sisters are crazy."

"They sound like fun," Zoe said, "and concerned."

"That concern is called being nosy." Will reached out and stuck his finger into the crease in Zoe's towel. He tugged but she stood her ground.

Zoe shook her head. She pulled away and Will issued a silent prayer that the towel would fall. He didn't think he'd ever get tired of seeing her body. The curves. The softness. The wetness.

"In less than thirty-six hours..." Zoe began.

"We'll be on our first date?" Will dropped his hand and stroked his face again, remembering he needed to shave. "Or are we going for round six tonight?"

"I believe we made it to round seven," Zoe said with

a wink. "I see why you have this TOP tattoo." Soft fingers brushed against the space above his heart.

"That's my fraternity."

Her perfect lips formed an O.

"Didn't you pledge anything in college?" There was something about the striped tube socks Zoe wore that gave him the image of her in a pledge line.

More of Zoe's hair spilled over her shoulders when she shook her head. "Did you forget I was a nerd?"

A nerd was the furthest thing from his mind.

"Well, I was. There weren't too many sorority girls asking me to join or any frat guys banging on my door to date me. The Greek life didn't work out for me."

The only person who was going to bang on her door from here on out was going to be him. He couldn't wait to see what her place looked like. Did she have the same kind of posters on her walls as she did in her childhood bedroom? "I'm looking forward to our date tonight."

"Tonight?" Zoe perked up.

"We can have our first date when we return to Miami," Will clarified. "And perhaps tonight I'll keep better track of how many times you climax."

"But then again, if tonight is our first date, I ought to behave. I wouldn't want you to get the wrong impression of me."

"You've already made an impression, baby."

Zoe stepped up and gave him a kiss on his chin. The soft feel of her tongue and nibble of her teeth fueled his erection. "I'll impress you more this afternoon."

"Speaking of this afternoon," Will groaned, "I am afraid my brothers are here, as well."

"A family affair?"

"Well, we are sponsoring all the makeup." Will lifted the lavender jar of lotion and opened the top. Slowly he dipped his finger into the creamy white center and pulled out a dollop on his finger, then swiped it across her bare shoulder. "Which means the only products you can use are Ravens."

"I can make that work." Zoe leaned her head to the side and kissed his thumb.

"And it should mean the only products on you should be Ravens."

Zoe dropped the towel. "What about putting a Ravens body part in me?"

And who was he to say no?

After a quick tryst in the shower, Zoe kissed Will goodbye and headed next door to the pageant. There was a nice-sized building off to the side of the hotel that was home to small concerts. Today it held fifty girls, all aiming to win the crown of Miss Southwood. Parents and children, fans and talent scouts already filled the seats. Children in fluffy dresses practiced their dance moves in the hallway and aisles. Older teens fiddled with their cell phones as they stood around in line, waiting for hair and makeup.

Zoe waved to her new friends, the production crew. Her feet barely hit the ground on her way to the beauty room. She and Will had plans for tonight. Zoe pushed the job out of her mind for now. Their future held nothing but excitement.

"Hey, Zoe," Lily exclaimed. "We're stuck over here." She waved a metallic fingernail file with a cream-colored handle in the air to catch Zoe's attention.

All the nail accessories and products at Lily's station bore the signature cream, gold and lavender colors of Ravens Cosmetics, but the dozens of bottles were filled with various bright colors, stemming from the brightest of pinks and neon blues, to the soft classic pale pink and even to a black. It was refreshing to see Ravens stepping to the plate to meet their competitors.

"Swanky digs you've got here," Zoe said with a low whistle. Ravens Cosmetics had gone all out to make sure their name was seen.

Lily nodded her head in agreement. "As is y'all's."

"Y'all's?"

"Sorry," Lily blushed. Zoe loved the shade of red on her cheeks. She clearly did not need any makeup. "I've been in Southwood too long. I meant you guys have a nice setup over there."

"Over there" meant a long station with at least six black chairs in front of makeup mirrors. Confusion clouded Zoe's head. She was under the impression she'd be the only makeup artist today. The pageant started at noon and she would have been working nonstop until at least four. A part of her was relieved to know she'd be able to give each contestant her full attention. As a professional she could get a job done in ten minutes.

"Zoe." Rebecca waved a gold curling iron with a pearl handle in Zoe's direction. "Hey, girl."

Zoe was in midwave when the man standing next to Rebecca turned around. She snarled when their eyes locked. "Titus."

"Zoe," he mouthed with utter disdain, then turned his attention to Rebecca. "So, you two are supposed to be friends now?"

Rebecca's soft smile didn't ease the situation. "We're friends, Titus. Stop being rude."

"I'll stop being rude when she stops thinking she brought eighties makeup back by telling everyone I copied her."

Her upper lip curled, Zoe's body heated from the blood boiling in anger and with her fists clenched she stalked forward. "Why are you even here?"

"Uh, it looks like I'm about to show Ravens Cosmetics that I'm their new Creative Design Director." In usual Titus fashion, he did a dramatic spin. His black smock twirled around his large frame.

"I don't understand," Zoe snapped.

"You didn't think you were going to keep the CEO's attention all to yourself?" Titus asked with his hands on his hip. "Luckily for me, the board found out about this little trip."

Suddenly Zoe remembered what Will had told her about half the board at Ravens. They wanted to see the company fail. Bringing Titus on certainly would do the job. She needed to talk to Will. Did he know what they were trying to do? Zoe absentmindedly reached to touch her good-luck pearls and remembered again that she hadn't brought them with her.

"Don't look so lost." Titus continued to gloat. "Once I am the CDD, I may hire you to consult on the Halloween special I plan on hosting."

Rebecca elbowed Titus in the gut and offered Zoe an apologetic smile. "Go gather your girls, Titus. Let Zoe get settled in her station."

It was then Zoe realized that her station was right next to Titus's. Photographs of the contestants were taped against their mirrors, lining the frames. Zoe went

over to her spot and peeked inside her beauty box.
Any bit of anger washed away. Lying in the center
of the lavender satin box was the soon-to-be-released
glitter lipstick from Ravens Zoe had been dying to
get her hands on. The lipstick was a two-part design,
one containing color, the other glitter. This was the
idea she'd been concocting for a while now, but it had
taken using several different products for one ultimate
look. Someone at Ravens had a great mind like her.
She couldn't wait to collaborate. A few celebrity faces
popped into mind, women who would love buying this
in one tube rather than combining lipsticks. Renewed
energy gushed through her veins. Zoe was armed with
all the tools she needed and was headed into battle.

The girls Zoe had been given were all under the age
of twenty. As with most pageants, there were age divi-
sions. All of the makeup artists were given girls from
each group. The Wee Peaches were between the ages
of one and five. Everyone had at least one Wee Peach
but Lexi insisted those girls be as natural as possible. The next division was the six-to-eleven age group.
These girls were given full glitz makeup if they wanted
it. This meant they could wear false lashes and false
teeth—or flippers, as they were called. Zoe hated to
admit that Titus's work was heavy but good. Zoe was
not too comfortable putting her signature wingtip on.
They were still little girls.

The contestants were broken down in ages somewhere between twelve and fifteen, and then sixteen
to twenty-six. All were dazzled with the makeup and
wanted more. Some of them were eager to sit in Zoe's
chair because their sisters had gotten their makeup
done for prom yesterday. Occasionally Titus stood by

and sneered. It didn't help that during her downtime, Rebecca shared photographs from last night's dinner. He muttered under his breath about how, if Zoe was given the position, he was sure he knew why. Titus even commented about the time stamp on each photograph and noticed that, at some point, Zoe and Will disappeared. This was exactly the kind of thing Lexi had warned her about.

By noon, the beauty portion of the pageant was on its way for the sixteen- to twenty-three-year-olds. Zoe enjoyed getting to know her girls and learning about them. She wanted each girl's makeup to be an expression of herself, rather than a painted face. In Zoe's eyes, none of the other artists were competition. But Titus went for the kill. He didn't care about the ages of the girls. He used the glitter gloss on each girl. Zoe was tempted, but she knew the colors were too mature for clients. And, unlike Titus, Zoe's groups of contestants were all under the age of sixteen. She overheard one of Titus's girls say she was twenty-six. A part of her wondered if this was part of the competition. Was Ravens Cosmetics looking for a way for the interviewees to integrate their new makeup line?

Everyone was able to take thirty to forty-five minutes for lunch. Everyone who worked backstage gathered around the long buffet table. Riddled with guilt, Zoe decided to give Lexi a call. She needed to know what she should do. Did she go against her morals of keeping young girls looking young or did she go full out to get the job? The cell service in the back was horrible.

Zoe went outside to get better reception. She headed over to the bridge for privacy and clarity. Lexi's phone went straight to voice mail, so Zoe decided to finish her walk, then she'd try again. She wondered if her father had ever made it out here to check out the view. At any point now, Zoe expected a call from him to give the go-ahead to bring her mom back. It wasn't like her mother didn't know about the proposal. He did it every year, just in different places.

The summer sun felt good on her face. Freezing air conditioning blasted in Zoe's station. It had to, in order to keep the girls from melting. Green leaves littered the walkway of the bridge over the lake. With everything there was to do this week, there hadn't been a lot of time for long strolls over the water. A low limb of a weeping willow blocked part of the way. As she grew closer the clear sound of a conversation grew louder. Zoe hesitated and wondered if she should turn around or try to walk through the group talking.

"So, how did Will take it when he found out we're backing his choice for the director by whomever he votes to win the pageant?"

Will? Zoe decided to stand still. Whoever was talking about Will—*her Will*—did not have a caring pitch to his tone. Through the leaves she spied three people: two men and a woman. All three had the height of the Ravens family. She wondered if these were some of the cousins Will warned her about.

"Charles, can you believe he told me and Dixon it was fine?" the woman said. She spoke as if her head were held high in the air, very snooty. "As if he has things under control. I can't stand him."

"Katie," the man named Charles answered, clapping his hands together, "we are so close to being done with this company, once and for all. We just need to focus."

"I promise you guys—forcing Will to choose this quickly is going to throw his game," said the man Zoe guessed was Dixon.

"I can't believe he has no idea we found Octavia." Charles rubbed his hands together manically.

A row of hairs rose on the back of Zoe's neck. Octavia Ravens? The missing heir?

"We'll just keep her under wraps until after the final vote. Grandma will be upset with the company, but we'll be the ones softening the blow when we bring our long-lost aunt home." Charles chuckled. "Let Grandma's favorite continue thinking he knows what he's doing."

"And we owe this to my fabulous sis." Dixon gave a silent round of applause. "If you hadn't broken your nail after trying to negotiate things at Pink Stilettos Cosmetics, we might never have had this opportunity." He gave a harrumph. "Will ain't the only one who can play hero."

"Oh, my God, don't get me started," Katie gasped. "Did you hear him talking about beat-faces and winged eyeliner? You would have thought he took a class."

Through the seething anger, Zoe's heart swelled with pride. So Will had been listening to her all this time.

"Whatever," a male voice said. "He still thinks he's going to be Grandma's savior."

"That's because he never had to work hard a day in his life," the woman sneered.

Well, Zoe shrugged, before knowing Will, she might have agreed there. But that didn't mean she agreed with whatever these people were saying. They truly were trying to ruin the company. Zoe turned around and headed back toward the pageant. She spied Will's broad shoulders immediately. He sat heads above the rest of the judges at their own booth with his back to her. A red velvet rope separated them from everyone else roaming around. If she had superpowers right now she'd use telepathy to get Will to turn around.

"You know I can't let you get any closer," said a security guard.

Zoe read the name tag of the man-wall. "I'm sorry, but Mr. Anderson, it's imperative that I speak with Will Ravens."

"And you can," the giant man turned Zoe around, "*after* the pageant."

"Fine." Zoe scooted off and realized she didn't have Will's cell phone number. She had last week, but was sure she'd thrown it away after her interview. Zoe swam upstream in the sea of mothers and daughters. A cloud of hairspray choked her and she had to stop and catch her breath for a moment.

"Zoe, right?"

Zoe glanced down at the beefy hand on her shoulder. She glanced up and tilted her head to the side, trying to recall the name of the man who'd let Will land his plane on his property. When she had met him he was wearing a pair of greasy overalls and now he wore a tailor-made dark-blue suit. Sharp, Zoe thought to herself.

"Dominic," he offered. "Will's frat brother. You guys were at my place earlier this week."

Earlier this week seemed more like a lifetime ago. "Hi, yes. How are you?"

"A bit out of place." Dominic chuckled. He slid his hands into his pockets and looked around. "This isn't really my speed."

"Yet, here you are." Zoe widened her eyes. She decided to skip the obvious. The man was here supporting his friend and checking out the women. "Are you enjoying yourself?"

"It's a bit insane," Dominic admitted with a quick nod of his head. He fanned away another cloud of hairspray from a mother spraying her young daughter as they rushed by. "I can't believe people willingly put themselves through an ordeal like this."

"All in the name of the crown," Zoe offered.

"That is the end game, right?"

"Say, how much do you know about what Will's going through at his company?"

Dominic extracted his hand from his pocket to scratch his chin. "You mean, about half the family wanting to shut down the operations?"

"That would be it," said Zoe. "Well, his cousins are here and I just overheard them plotting about his decision for today's contestant." She relayed the story, and Dominic listened with fierce intent. Clearly he cared for his friend. "And I can't get close enough to warn him."

"So you're afraid if he doesn't select your work as the overall winner, he's going to lose the company?"

The tone of his voice changed more into an accusation. Zoe took a step back. "Well, I…"

"Sounds to me like you may care more about your future job than his."

A jolt of embarrassment shocked Zoe's system. "I care a lot about Will."

"As long as you're in the running for this position he has to fill?"

It was then that Zoe realized Dominic's eyes were

a fiery light brown that practically glowed red with anger. "Hey, I think we got off on the wrong foot here. If you're asking me if I want the job as Creative Design Director, well, the answer is hell yes. I'm sure you're just looking out for your frat brother here, but I can assure you I could get any job that I want."

Dominic crossed his arms across his wide chest, making him look even larger. "So you wouldn't care if he doesn't pick you today?"

"He's already picked me," Zoe snapped.

"Well then, you have nothing to worry about."

A set of identical twin women were returning to their seats and stopped at the sound of Zoe's declarations. She had no doubt in the world these were Will's sisters. The lights dimmed. So much for trying to get hold of Will.

Chapter 11

Will glanced down at the score sheet once again. He had no idea what in the hell half the items on the lists meant. He was supposed to rate these ladies and young girls on a scale of one to ten in several categories. Evening gowns, hair, smiles, makeup, talent and technique. What did he know about any of those?

Technique? No one fell off the stage. A few girls tripped while tap dancing and some hit the wrong note while singing, but other than that, Will didn't know what he was supposed to do. Sasha, who sat beside him on the right, scribbled over her sheets with each contestant. Vera, on his left, did the same. She made notes, smiley faces and even drew the devil on one girl's page. Kathleen, at the very edge of the table, already had her paperwork stacked together with her hands folded on top. Kahlil leaned forward and gave him a head nod. They were in the same boat. Sort of. Will knew what was at stake.

According to the meeting held after he left Zoe's side this morning, his scores determined who received the Creative Design Director position. Zoe's future was in his hands. Besides his immediate family coming to Southwood for the pageant, the anti-cousins had arrived, as well. They were tired of the position lingering unfilled and wanted him to make a quick decision. Katie and Dixon were smug with their demands, stating that as members of the board, they had a right to make him choose.

So far he hadn't seen anything too crazy and over-the-top to make him think any of the numerous girls walking across the stage were done up by Zoe. He studied the eyeliner, but it seemed as if every other girl wore the winged look. It wasn't until a contestant blew a kiss into the crowd that Will found his winner. The crowd loved her. Will liked her makeup. And to add icing to this cake, the girl wore the glittered lipstick the same way Zoe had applied it to the prom girls at Magnolia Palace and most importantly, the dramatic wing tip. He teetered on the contestant with the modest beauty, but after last night and this morning, Will set aside his morals. He needed Zoe near him.

To be sure he chose right, Will glanced at the other score sheets whenever the other judges came across the same girl. Everyone gave her high scores, except for the beauty queen seated next to him. Vera had been generous, even to the girl who dropped her baton, which was on fire, giving her a higher score than she did Will's favorite. He was more confident that the other beauty queen, Kathleen, liked the same girl, too.

"Are we all settled on who the winner is?" asked Kathleen.

Will, along with everyone else at the table, nodded. The houselights dimmed. There were girls and parents seated beside him at the judges' table. Will doodled on a piece of paper as the names were called for each category and age range. The young girls went first. Winners were called by special titles. Everyone got a small trophy for participation and then crowns were given to the winners in those groups. There were awards for the prettiest smile, friendliest contestant and most helpful. The runner-up princess of each category received a sizable tiara. But they had to go through this for each group. At this rate, Will wasn't going to get back to Miami until late, and he still had plans to be with Zoe tonight, with or without her as Ravens Cosmetics's newest employee.

Finally it was time to crown Miss Southwood Glitz. The top three women stood dressed in sparkling ball gowns—pink, blue and yellow—on the stage, clutching hands. They'd changed into their evening gowns. The winner, as the emcee explained, would travel across the county and represent Southwood in the official Miss South Georgia pageant in December.

The pageant contentants were narrowed down from fifty to ten girls, and then down to five left on the stage. Each girl drew questions written by one of the judges from a clear fishbowl. The five were slimmed down to three final contestants. Will was glad his question wasn't chosen. He'd wanted to know if any of the ladies had a superpower, what it would be. He would definitely wish for the power of transportation. He'd be anywhere else but here—with Zoe.

December. Will zoned out with the idea of Zoe. He wondered what he'd get Zoe for the holidays. Would they stay in Miami or visit someplace cold? Without thinking, Will wiggled his eyebrows at the idea of stretching out in front of a fireplace with Zoe.

"And the second runner-up…" the emcee said into the microphone.

Second? Leaning forward, Will shook his head and blinked into focus and realized there were just two girls on stage. His daydream of Zoe had caused him to miss the final three going to answer the same question from the emcee. They faced each other, clutching hands for dear life.

"Second runner-up is Miss Cupcakery."

The audience screamed with applause. Miss Cupcakery was whisked away by a few ushers. The reigning Miss Southwood placed a crown on top of Miss Restoration's head and the queen began her walk across the stage. His choice won.

The applause of the audience was deafening. The other judges at the table mouthed congratulations and shook hands. Will glanced around the stage. The other contestants surrounded the new Miss Southwood. The behind-the-scenes staff peered through the curtains. Will shifted in his seat for a glimpse of Zoe and her purple smock. The spotlight caught her golden hoop earrings, visible beneath her hair, piled on top of her head in a messy bun. Will's heart seized.

"Zoe," he breathed her name and began to rise from his seat.

A set of heavy hands clamped down on Will's back. At the moment, the only person Will wanted to see was Zoe and perhaps the person she was about to hug. He needed to make sure she hugged the winner and held her hand in the air like a true boxing champ and coach. Every step she took agonized Will. Mothers and little girls were stopping her to take selfies. Teens stopped her for a photograph. Beauty queens who hadn't won covered their faces with their hands and Zoe helped each one stop their mascara from running. All he needed to see was who Zoe had teamed up with, just to make sure she was the one who'd secured the spot at Ravens Cosmetics.

He needed her to win to prove his cousins wrong. Zoe had been right. She was the best thing for the company.

"Young William!" Eva screamed in his ear as she came up behind him and wrapped her arms around his shoulders.

"Will," Charles said, strolling into his line of view. An annoyed sigh escaped Will's throat. It came out more like a growl and with the crowd's applause slowing down, it was apparently heard by his cousin. Charles's eyes stretched wide. "Let's see your score sheets."

"No need," Will retorted, still shoving his paperwork in his cousin's direction. "She's about to hug the winner now." Sure of himself, Will cocked his head to the side and nodded toward the stage...and that's when he realized he'd been too sure too quickly. Zoe stood off with the second runner-up, dabbing underneath the girl's lashes with a tissue.

"Rather rude of you," Charles said, looking toward the stage where a large bald man in a lavender smock and white boots hugged the new Miss Southwood.

What the hell? Will asked himself.

"Fantastic," Charles said, clapping his hands. "I'll go let him know right now."

Will rose again to get to Zoe, but another hand clapped onto his shoulder. Will shrugged off the grip and turned around. For a moment he didn't recognize his frat brother, Dominic. At least there was one friendly face, someone who didn't want something from him. "Hey, man."

"Hey, great job." Dominic nodded his head at the commotion on stage.

"Why didn't you tell me you were into pageant shows? Is this your way of picking up women now?"

Dominic shrugged his shoulders. "It's not what you think." At the same time, a few ladies waved like schoolchildren in his direction. Dominic turned to watch them leave, and when he turned back, Will gave him a raised brow. "I swear," Dominic laughed. "I am sponsoring a contestant."

The questions flooded Will's brain. He started with the first one. "What?"

Dominic rubbed his chin. "Well, Alisha suggested I bond with the community better. Apparently, my up-scale shop matches my attitude."

One thing Will had enjoyed when Dominic's family came to visit them. Dominic was the oldest and his baby sister followed them around. Will, never having had a younger sister, found her charming. If Alisha thought Dominic needed to change things, she was probably right.

"In other words, the town thinks you're stuck-up." It couldn't have been further than the truth, but Will understood how Dominic might give the wrong impression. Maybe if his frat brother showed off more of his tattoos, the people would find him down-to-earth. "So, which one did you sponsor?"

"The winner, Miss Restoration, as in Crowne's Restoration."

Will raked his hands over his head. Blood pounded in his ears. "I didn't even put two and two together."

Dominic's girl had won; meanwhile, his lost. Jesus, what had he done?

From Zoe's vantage point on the stage she watched Will and his best friend shake hands. She tried to focus on the girls wanting to take a picture with her, but her mind was spinning. If what she'd overheard was true, she'd just lost her opportunity for the position she most desired. Titus, clearly knowing what was at stake, hugged his winning contestant and gave Zoe a smug wink. Through it all, Zoe kept a smile on her face. She had to. Everyone kept asking for a photograph.

With each picture her mind wandered. How did this happen? She had no Plan B. After the last of the girls and their mothers finished taking pictures, a man dressed in a suit approached her. She'd seen him before. There was something familiar about him. His features were very Ravens-esque and then it hit her. This was Charles, whom she'd spied on through the weeping willow leaves.

"Miss Baldwin," the man said, with his hand outstretched. "Allow me to introduce myself."

The badge around his neck already told her who he was. "Mr. Ravens."

"Charles Ravens," he replied. "We haven't had the pleasure to meet."

"No, we haven't." Zoe tried. She wanted to be

friendly, but this man's vendetta against his cousin had cost her a job. Her dream job.

"I've been a fan of yours for a while now." Charles held on to Zoe's hand for a few seconds too long.

Zoe pulled her arm back and shoved her hands into the front of her smock. She fiddled with the tube of lipstick from the beauty box. Her downfall. Maybe she should have used it like Titus had.

"I wanted to come over here and let you know that we at Ravens Cosmetics appreciate you applying to our company and we'll keep your name on file," Charles went on.

"That's kind of you." Zoe glanced over at Will. Electricity jolted her body when their eyes locked. He stopped his conversation with Dominic and made his way toward her, not caring who he bumped into. "I appreciate the opportunity."

What else was she supposed to say? What else was she supposed to do? Fall on the ground like one of the younger contestants who hadn't gotten the trophy she wanted? The redeeming factor in all of this was Will. Her heart swelled with…love. Love? The room spun. How had this happened? It was too fast, right? She couldn't believe it. All the noise around her ceased. The only thing she heard was the beating of her heart…the beating of her heart and Will's footsteps as he neared her. She needed to tell him. She loved him.

"I hope I'm not interrupting anything." Will reached Zoe with arms outstretched. He took hold of her forearm, then wrapped her against his frame.

Zoe blinked him into focus. "Not at all."

Charles's eyes darted toward the tender touch. His lips pressed together and Zoe was sure he *hmm*ed under his breath. "I was telling Miss Baldwin about her wonderful work and how we'll keep her résumé on file."

The grip around her waist tightened and Will cleared his throat. He wasn't letting her go. "Once again, thanks, Charles, for doing my job for me."

"Well, you were busy with your frat brother. Ah, here he comes now."

In the brief moment when Charles lifted his head above Will's shoulder, Will leaned over. "Zoe, I need to explain something."

"Don't worry about it." Swallowing past the lump in her throat, Zoe shrugged her shoulders. "I second-guessed myself and Titus was better today when it counted."

"I'll figure something out," Will whispered with a kiss at her temple.

More than anything she wanted to tell Will what she'd realized, but her words were lost when Dominic came over, Titus and the new Miss Southwood Glitz in tow. Zoe remembered the woman's name was Waverly. She was a former Miss Something who'd lost her other crown due to bad behavior.

"Zoe, you remember Dominic Crowne?" Will asked, his hand on her lower back.

For a millisecond, Zoe and Dominic stared each other down. He gave a lopsided smirk and a head nod.

Waverly stepped forward and shook Zoe's hand. "You're awesome, Miss Zoe. It was a real pleasure to meet you this afternoon. I am a huge fan."

"But you work better with me." Titus brought up the rear. His smugness was enough to knock Zoe off the stage.

Zoe's eyes darted between the four of them stand-

ing in front of her. The dots began to align. Now she
recalled why Will hadn't cared about her getting the
Creative Design Director's position. He already had
something in mind.

"This is cozy." Charles cleared his throat. "Titus,
you must be familiar with Zoe Baldwin."

"We've met," Zoe and Titus belted out with the same
amount of animosity in their voices.

"I can't thank you enough for this opportunity, Mr.
Ravens," Waverly gushed, shaking Will's and then
Charles's hands. "And Mr. Ravens."

Zoe stepped backward but Will's hold on her waist
kept her from leaving. "Everything okay?"

"No," Zoe whispered.

"Dom was just talking about all of us getting together for a celebration," said Will. "What do you say
we hang back here for one day?" He leaned close to
whisper in her ear. "Tonight can still be our first date."

Pain ached in her ribs. "Honestly," Zoe began
slowly, "I'm all packed. I might as well head back tonight and I already have my ticket."

"So you'll fly back with me on the company plane."
Will moved closer. "Like when we came here."

A lifetime ago, Zoe thought. She shot a glance at
Dominic, not sure why he made her so nervous. Probably because he already knew what Zoe wanted and
knew the plans he'd already made with Will for the
winner. How long had they been conspiring? Did Will
plan on making Waverly a winner before he learned
of the company's plans to hire the makeup artist who
did the winner's face?

A piercing pang pinched the bridge of Zoe's nose.
Tears were threatening. She needed to get away from

here. Disappointment hit her harder than she expected. She needed to go home and made up a lie. "No, forgot I have things I need to do tomorrow."

"Zoe?" Will questioned her with a raised brow. He was confused, as he should be. Zoe knew he had no idea she was aware of his plans for hire. But, then again, she'd known all along he didn't want her. Zoe choked out a sob. After he met with his cousins, did he meet up with Dominic and make plans for his contestant to win? This is what fraternity members did, right? Help each other out? How easy had it been for Will to come up with a decision on the position after swearing he needed to think long and hard? Will's face softened, his lips frowned. "What is it?"

"I've got to go, Will." Zoe stepped backward. "I've got to get back. Please excuse me. And congratulations, Waverly. You were truly lovely."

At some point after midnight Zoe returned to the comfort of her home. Usually she wasn't on the verge of tears when she returned, but dropping her keys on the ground nearly set her off. The extra weight of emotions drained her. This was clearly not her day, her month—hell, even her year. Zoe rushed inside her apartment before her sobs could wake the Dohertys next door.

Even though she had only been on the company plane one time, Zoe already missed it. She wondered what would have been better, flying last week seated next to the fake LL Cool J or being seated tonight with someone who could have been a heavyweight wrestler. Zoe's bones ached from being wedged against the window.

Leaving her suitcase by the door, Zoe trotted over

to the kitchen, kicking out of her red flip-flops. Before leaving for the airport she had been able to change out of her smock and slip into a red-and-white-striped maxi dress. As much as she wanted to shower after her flight, Zoe's stomach growled. She was famished and the refrigerator had no answers for her. Like déjà vu, Zoe's cell phone rang and Prince came over the speaker. This was the same scenario as when Lexi had invited her to come back to Southwood. Zoe had been heartbroken over Ravens Cosmetics and she was starving. The two differences this time were that Zoe let the phone ring and she had no food in her fridge. Zoe closed the refrigerator door and let the call go to voice mail.

No one on the van ride to Atlanta could believe Zoe hadn't stayed in Southwood for one more evening with Will. Kenzie, the main person rooting for a union between Will and Zoe, asked everyone to cut Zoe some slack. Luke sat in the van and ticked off a list of the places he freelanced for that were interested in her work for the same position. Zoe needed to come up with a new plan, and this time it might include having to move and try resettling someplace else. She sighed heavily and reached for the stack of mail on her counter, still hating the idea of leaving. Where else would she find a neighbor willing to drop off her mail while she was out of town?

A soft knock came at the door. She figured it was either Mr. or Mrs. Doherty, coming to check on her after all the noise she'd made coming inside. Without thinking, she opened the door. It took several blinks for her eyes to adjust to the image in front of her.

On top of her heart breaking, it now melted. Will, still in his suit, leaned against the jamb. The first three buttons at his neck were undone and the tie hung loose. A rustle of plastic caught her attention. Down by his side he held a takeout bag sporting the red, black and white of the Trinidad and Tobago flag.

"You went to Trudy's?"

"I called it in. We were supposed to have our first official date when we got back to Miami, Zoe," Will said with a calm voice. "We couldn't decide on Monday or tonight, so I chose now."

"I'm not hungry," she lied. The delicious scents caused her mouth to water.

"I don't understand. I didn't peg you for a sore loser."

Of all the audacity in the world! Zoe's mouth widened as a few choice words came to mind about Will and his nerve. "Sore loser?" she hissed. "How did you even know what apartment I live in?" The locks on her neighbor's door clicked and Patrick Doherty poked his red head out. "Sorry to wake you, Patrick."

"Everything okay?"

For a moment Zoe wondered if she needed to get rid of Will. He may have arrived with dinner but the way his eyes bored into her soul unnerved her. "I'm okay, thanks for asking."

After a reluctant few seconds, filled with five-foot-eight Patrick sizing up Will's six-four frame, her neighbor nodded and went back inside his place. Zoe stepped back and allowed plenty of space for Will to enter her apartment.

"Your address was on your résumé," Will answered her. As he passed, she couldn't help but be mesmerized by his powerful stride. He went straight to the open kitchen and set the bag down. Fragrant aromas from the Trinidadian chicken stew filled the air.

Despite the rumble in her stomach, Zoe leaned against the counter and folded her hands. "Why are you here?"

"We have a date." Will helped himself to a view inside her refrigerator and shook his head. "This is funny."

"You're mocking the contents of my fridge?" Zoe squared her shoulders.

"I'm laughing at yet another thing we have in common." Will widened the door. "We have matching contents."

Zoe rolled her eyes to keep from grinning.

Will closed the door and turned to lean over the counter. He covered her hands with his. "I'm sorry with the way things ended with the CDD position, Zoe."

"It is what it is. And you warned me you weren't interested in my work." The key word in there was "work." There was no doubting his attraction to her. Zoe thought about her newly discovered feelings. Somehow, this was not the moment to confess she was in love with him. Anger and disappointment still seethed within.

"Don't act like that," said Will. "The board put the restrictions on me this morning. They specified that the makeup artist who did the winner would get the position. I've watched you work with the staff and crew at Magnolia Palace and I've learned to appreciate your work. I even was sure I knew your work. I looked for all the ladies with the drastic winged liner you do. I was sure Waverly was yours."

"Well, she wasn't," Zoe snapped. "She was Titus's. Of all people, she was Titus's."

"So are you mad at me for not voting the right person?" Will asked, squeezing her hand. His dark eyes pleaded with hers.

Zoe tried to jerk her hand away but he held on to her. "Oh," she chuckled sarcastically, "I believe you picked the person you wanted to pick."

"Zoe, I looked for everything you taught me over the past few days." He let go of her hand and ticked off on his fingers the things he'd learned. "She even had the glittery mixed-matched lipstick thing you've been doing."

"That was from Ravens Cosmetics," Zoe grunted. "I thought you gave that to us on purpose. The products were great for women, but not the group of young girls I was assigned."

Will shook his head. "How in the hell was I supposed to do that? I wasn't allowed to see you all day."

"It was in the beauty box from your company," she gritted through her teeth. Realizing this wasn't going anywhere, Zoe took a step backward. "You know what? It doesn't even matter anymore. Titus won and your frat brother won. That's why you knew all along I wasn't going to get the position."

Will stood back as well and held his hands in the air in surrender. "Hold up. I had no idea Titus and Waverly would be paired up or that Dominic decided to sponsor a beauty queen. The whole point of the separation from the contestants was so that we didn't fraternize."

"Funny you mentioned frats. That's not the vibe I got from Dominic."

"Wait, when did you talk to Dom?" Will rushed to Zoe's side. "Did he say something that bothered you?"

"He didn't have to." Zoe avoided Will's touch. "He alluded to it enough. I just wish you would have told me."

Will didn't take her attempt to brush him off well. He stepped even closer. So close, she backed up against the archway leading into the living room. Using the back of his knuckles he caressed her cheek. "I'm not sure what's going on here. I didn't know Dom was sponsoring anyone until after the pageant. Talk to me."

Zoe hated herself for melting. There were plenty of jobs she had gotten in the past and she didn't need anyone to comfort her like this. But being here with him was different. If what he said was true, then there was no moment of conspiring against her or favoritism. Zoe's eyes stung from the overwhelming sensation of feeling foolish. "Look, I get not getting the job. I can handle it. It just stings that it's to someone like Titus. I'm bitter."

"You're not mad at me?" Warm breath brushed against her nose when Will chuckled. "But bitter over Titus?"

Not appreciating his laughter, Zoe pushed his chest away. "You're laughing at my pain?"

"No. Just your honesty."

Zoe moved toward the living room, all too aware of Will hot on her tail. She tried to focus on the bookshelves across the room on the wall, but only thought strangely of future photographs of the two of them, like at Lexi's from her and Stephen's wedding. "Something I figured you would appreciate."

Will wrapped his arms around her from behind. The

bitterness slowly thawed. His forearms were cradled beneath her breasts and lifted the stress of their weight and her emotions. Zoe leaned into him, willingly allowing him to lead her to the sleet-gray couch. Chills ran down her spine from the feathery touch of his fingertips. "What can I do to make it up to you?"

Zoe turned in to him. "Hire anyone else but Titus."

"What is the deal with you and Titus?"

"Nothing other than the man not having an original thought in his brain." Zoe wrapped her arm around Will's shoulders. Her fingers splayed against the curly hairs at the nape of his neck. She pushed out an irritated sigh. "You say a lot of the contestants had the same winged eyeliner and the glitter lips, right?"

"Yes."

"Titus has been stealing every design I do. That's why my designs on certain celebrities are so elaborate. I make them impossible for Titus to copy without getting caught, but as you know, no everyday woman walks around with a couture face."

"Why didn't you tell me any of this before?" Will stroked Zoe's thigh.

"And sound like I'm a complainer?" Zoe shook her head, letting it rest on his shoulder. The beat of his heart comforted her pain. "I respect your decision. I'm resilient. I'll make other plans."

Will pulled his head back, and wrinkles marred his perfect face. "Other plans?"

"The reason I went after the Creative Design Director position is because I wanted something permanent in Miami."

Will stroked Zoe's left arm and trailed it down to

her hand where they locked fingers. "You're not thinking about leaving here, are you?"

"I don't know," Zoe said with a shrug. "I have a few weeks to think about it."

"Good," Will said, maneuvering Zoe so her back rested against his chest. "I have a few weeks to convince you to stay in Miami."

Large hands stroked the swell of her breast and moved down toward her belly. Zoe moaned. The material of her dress crept up her legs as Will pulled it up. "I have a few jobs out of town," Zoe moaned in between sharp breaths. "But if I want to do anything in beauty, I've got to go somewhere else. Ravens Cosmetics holds the monopoly on practically everything in South Florida."

"You're leaving me?"

"Well, not right now." Zoe turned to tilt her face to his.

Something about their mouths meeting, something felt right. Something felt like home. Zoe purred. His hands stirred at the apex of her legs. The panties she wore were instantly wet. Slightly embarrassed, Zoe—as much as she hated to—pushed Will's hand away. "Will," she moaned. "I just got off the plane. I haven't showered."

Instead of listening to her, Will's index finger circled her nub. The length of his middle finger slipped deep inside. Zoe bucked her hips forward and, obliging, Will pressed his palm against her, grinding against her flesh. The other hand slipped the through the V of her dress and freed her breast.

Ecstasy consumed her. Heated blood boiled her bones. Zoe tried to get her thoughts together but it was hard, as hard as the erection pressing against her back. Will rubbed deeper, harder. His mouth skillfully worked hers and branded him on her. Their tongues reunited with a spark. Will used his legs to keep her legs spread wide. Moisture dripped from her body. She heaved, bounced and eventually rested her feet against the coffee table for leverage. Will hit the right spot over and over. Zoe broke the kiss. Her hands gripped the fabric of her couch and steadied herself with the right rhythm. Will pressed his lips against her earlobes and began to suck, and Zoe's body went crazy. She cried out for him over and over with each orgasmic wave.

"And now we shower," Will whispered into her ear before sweeping her up into his arms.

Chapter 12

In the few weeks after Zoe and Will returned to Miami, they tried to have a normal relationship, but it was damn near impossible for Will to have Zoe to himself for more than a couple of days at a time. She'd flown out to LA for a celebrity wedding right after they returned from Southwood. Then they had two full days together, which they spent in her apartment without ever leaving the facilities. Right after that she drove up to Orlando for the annual MET Awards, where she was surrounded by celebrities, all of whom gave Zoe a shout-out when they won an award or gave her name when interviewed on the red carpet. Will hoped her excessive traveling while they developed their relationship would make her want to stay. According to Zoe, her parents maintained a long-distance relationship. Zoe swore she never wanted that for herself.

"I feel like I haven't seen you in forever," Zoe wailed on her side of the FaceTime connection.

Will glanced down at his blotter calendar. After this Labor Day weekend, Zoe would be in New York for Fashion Week. If she felt like they hadn't seen each other much since they returned from Southwood, it was going to be even busier in the next few months.

"Me, too." Will tried to sound excited, when deep down inside he was equally frustrated. She'd warned him that her life was hectic. He understood now why she wanted something more permanent and he hated himself for not being the one to give it to her. "You don't have my face as the screen saver on your phone?" The moment he said that, the five-minute timer on his computer screen expired and the selfie Zoe had taken of the two of them together out on her balcony filled the screen. Will pressed the space bar and brought up the projected figures in spreadsheets for Ravens Cosmetics.

"You're cute," Zoe said drily.

"And even cuter in person," Will added. "Speaking of which, when do I get to see you?"

"You're seeing me now." Zoe laughed and blew him a kiss.

"I meant naked in my bed."

A pretty shade of red brushed across her cheeks. Someone near her laughed. A flutter shook his heart with the idea of her on the Fisher Island Ferry, heading toward his home on the barrier island neighborhood. She was close. "Where are you?" he asked, looking at the images behind her. She must have been sitting with her back against a wall.

"I'm not alone but I was heading toward your place."

Knowing she was this close, he felt excitement flush him. The hands on the grandfather clock in his office slowly ticked away toward five, but since it was Friday, why the hell *not* kick the weekend off early? Half the support staff had left already, including Will's secretary. So keeping up with everyone else, Will pulled his briefcase out from under his desk. This weekend they were going to have time together. Will had made arrangements to have everything they needed at the tips of their fingers in his home. He toyed with the idea of having a personal masseuse but broke the pencil in his hand in half at the idea of someone else touching her body.

"Give me forty-five minutes and be naked when I get there."

"Will—" Zoe pleaded.

Not wanting to hear a protest, Will slid his finger to the red icon and disconnected the line just in time. The door to his office pushed open without a knock. Donovan and Marcus entered.

"Hey, little brother," Marcus said, taking a seat. "Zoe must be in town."

Since the pageant, there had been no way to keep his relationship with Zoe quiet. Eva and Dana were already hounding him about when to have a wedding and whether he and Zoe wanted it in spring or summer. In his last email from Dana, she'd wanted permission to contact Jamerica Baldwin, Zoe's mother. It wasn't quite permission but more of a reminder that Dana still had modeling contacts she could use to get in touch with her. Right now, Will found the way his sisters teased him amusing. Nothing was set in stone. Will hadn't even broached the idea of marriage with

Zoe. Hell, compared with the intimate time at Magnolia Palace, the two of them barely spent any time together.

"What makes you think Zoe's in town?" Will asked.

Donovan snorted and elbowed Marcus in the ribs. He leaned back in his seat and propped his feet on Will's desk. "You're about to pack up and leave for the day."

"It's so cute," Marcus mocked. He lifted his fingers in the air and pretended to pinch Will's cheeks from across the room. "Don, you remember a few months ago when Will burned the midnight oil every night?"

"Is there something the two of you wanted?" Will asked. He kicked his briefcase back under his desk.

"We don't want to alarm you," said Donovan, "but the board just called an emergency meeting."

Will swore under his breath. "What now?"

"I couldn't get anything out of Charles or Brandon," Marcus began, "but Dixon's secretary has been pulling the data for the online work from Titus."

The online magazine was Titus's field. The new CDD of Ravens Cosmetics had sunk a lot of money into technology for people to order their cosmetics and products via their website. Because Titus held a tech degree, Will trusted him to sweeten the site.

"And you know this how?" Will asked with a slow drawl. What ran through his mind was a potential lawsuit. They were beginning to run out of single women working at Ravens.

As usual, Marcus smiled smugly and leaned back in his chair. "Don't you worry your pretty little head over that. Your big brother is handling things."

Will decided to ignore the mental list of corporate crimes sounding off in his head with the illegal implications of what Marcus said. The last thing they needed was a lawsuit. "I'll buy you a drink for taking one for the team."

"No worries. It was actually my pleasure." Marcus shrugged his shoulders. "She was pretty hot and flexible. I think she only missed the Olympics in Brazil due to a hurt back. But her back is fine now," Marcus concluded with a sheepish wink.

Rather than listening to his brother's escapades, Will preferred hearing the news. He cleared his throat and gained his brothers' attention. "What did you find out about the data she'd been collecting?"

"It was data on the Creative Design Director, the one *you* handpicked," said Marcus, reminding Will of a choice he would never live down. "What were you thinking?"

"Me?" Will gasped. "You were at the impromptu board meeting where they said whoever styled the winner of the pageant I voted for would get the CDD position."

"Which you still got wrong," Marcus reminded him—something he reminded Will of every time they got together. This included the moment before Titus had attended his very first meeting. "Zoe was perfect for the job."

"And now she's perfect for Will." Donovan chuckled.

"Can we get back to this meeting?" Will asked, resisting the urge to pinch the bridge of his nose to ward off an oncoming headache.

"Let's try more like, go to the meeting."

Tonight's plans were inevitably going to be put off. Will sent Zoe a text, pushed himself away from his desk and decided to dial Zoe's cell to let her know he would be running late.

Zoe's voice filled the screen before her face. "Are you trying to find out if I'm naked or not?"

Donovan and Marcus playfully leaped over the table. Will stood back against the window behind his desk. He held on to the phone while warding off his brothers with one hand. "Sorry, Zoe, I'm not alone now."

"Zoe," Marcus yelled out.

"When are you saving Ravens Cosmetics?" Donovan asked.

"Who needs saving?" Zoe bantered back. "I'm the one running around here from coast to coast. Need I remind you that one or both of you told me that Creative Design Director position was mine?"

"Sorry," both men sang.

"But it was Will's fault," Donovan blurted out.

Zoe's easy smile proved why Will loved her so much. She didn't hold a grudge and had wished Titus well on his first day. Zoe made it clear she didn't want to hear too much about how great Titus was or wasn't doing, but she supported the company because she genuinely wanted what was best.

"I was calling," Will said, shrugging away from his brothers' grasps, "to let you know I am going to be late. The board has called some emergency meeting."

"Everyone's here," Marcus called out.

"Including the young ones," Donovan finished.

"Sounds ominous," Zoe said, breaking eye contact with Will. He wondered for a moment if this was something she wished, but pushed the thought away. "Well, try to stay positive. I'll see you in a little bit."

The three brothers headed off toward the corner office of Ravens Cosmetics. This reminded Will of walking through a stadium ready to hit the field for a match. In soccer he'd prepared himself by working out and doing a lot of strength training and conditioning. Will readied himself for a match by studying his opponents. This meeting was far worse. His opponents were family members out for blood.

The glass walls of the conference room gave a clear view of the board: the Ravens. His blood. Will straightened his red tie with tiny magnolia flowers sprinkled on it. The tie was a gift from Zoe so he wouldn't forget about her. Not a chance. Will resisted smirking. He didn't want the anti-cousins, all facing him when he walked in, to get any sense of his emotions.

Instead of the stoic faces Will expected to see, most of the anti-cousins sat with knowing smirks. Katie, Dixon, Charles, Oscar, Mari, Thea and Brandon looked like the cats who'd devoured the canaries. This didn't worry Will. What bothered him, as he, Donovan and Marcus took their seats, was seeing Cora and J.J., Uncle Charles's wayward son. School should have already started and they needed to be in their dorms. Cora avoided eye contact with Will, and J.J. drummed his fingers on the glass cover of the black oak table. The beat stopped once the three brothers sat down on the same side as both sets of twins. Seven against seven.

"So, what brings all of us here today?" Will asked.

Dixon spoke first. Well, rather shoved a thick, legal-sized binder toward the center of the table. "This has been the data for the last twelve weeks of our e-commerce with your Creative Design Director in place."

A twitch threatened at the back of Will's jawline. "Alright?"

"Your golden choice failed to bring in tweaks, changes," said Dixon, referring to Titus once again. Nothing had improved after bringing Titus on board. The fans Will thought would follow Titus failed to support the hire. "As a matter of fact, our online sales have been cut in half and we've been steadily losing our subsidiaries left and right."

"What is this supposed to mean?" Marcus asked. "If these smaller companies are buying back their titles, we're still making money."

"For the love of God, you guys," Thea hissed, "we're getting off this sinking ship. It's time you all faced the truth."

"What truth?" Dana scoffed "That you guys are a bunch of lazy, entitled brats who don't know a thing about hard work?"

Thea's purple sculpted nails scraped against the glass and she rolled her eyes and fluttered what Will had come to know were wispy, catlike false lashes. "Said the prima donna model who used the company plane to get lobster from Maine." Thea paused for a moment, long enough for everyone to hear the audible sound of Dana closing her mouth. "Yeah, I saw the books. You're not modeling anymore, so there's no reason for the flight other than your sister's Key West lobsters not being good enough for you."

"Hey," Eva drawled with a scowl.

"You don't have the votes to shut Ravens down," Donovan declared with his intimidating, booming voice.

Cora squeaked, her face turning bright red. She

turned to look away but a tear fell down her face. Will knew at that moment it was over for Ravens Cosmetics. His heart fell. His shoulders slumped and a knot formed in his throat. He'd failed.

"Why are we bothering with conversation?" Charles asked. His gloating smirk was enough to make Will want to leap over the table and punch it off his face. "We're demanding a vote right now."

"How can you do this to Grandma?" Naomi asked. Her voice cracked with a hint of crying. Her twin reached over and patted her back. Will and his brothers clenched their fists.

Joyce spoke up. "It's plain and simple," she began. "Tell us how much it would take to buy you guys out."

With a quick calculation in his head, Will already knew they couldn't come up with the funds to buy them out at what he expected to be their inflated going rate. But Brandon surprised him the most with his response.

"We're done having our name attached to the sinking ship," said Brandon. "You think we want to stay if for some strange reason you guys pull a rabbit out of your hats and turn this around?"

"And if we even thought about selling the company to you guys," said Mari, another anti-cousin, "how do you think you'll look in the eyes of Grandma Naomi? We want to present it to her as if we made a group decision."

"That's not our concern," Donovan said. "We're the ones here on a daily basis."

"We're not selling to you," said Oscar. "We're dissolving the company. We have the votes."

The only thing Will could do was close his eyes and pray for a miracle. They needed to be saved. Grandma's birthday was next week. Was the family truly going to sit in the same room and tell her they'd dissolved the company? Her child? Her baby? How was he supposed to look his grandmother in the eyes and tell her he failed? The news was sure to kill her.

Will couldn't breathe. The air around him became stagnant. All he wanted to do was jump across the table and break one of their faces. If he moved to do so, he wasn't sure he'd be able to stop.

Before anyone had a chance to speak their minds, the conference door opened. Zoe entered. Confused, but still a gentleman, Will rose to his feet. All the men did. The receptionist from the front desk stormed breathlessly after Zoe.

"I'm so sorry for barging in like this," Zoe said.

"I tried to tell her y'all were in a meeting."

"It's okay, Tracey," said Donovan.

Will moved around the table to greet Zoe with a kiss on the cheek while she and Tracey faced off in the war of smirks. "What's going on, Zoe?"

"We're in a meeting," said Katie, rising to her feet with her arms across her chest. "A family meeting."

"Key word, 'family,'" Dixon enunciated.

In true Zoe-dramatic form, Zoe pressed her hand to her chest and took a bow. Will bit back a proud grin. "Well, I do apologize for interrupting this family meeting, but since you said it's a family thing..." She waltzed back over to the door and opened it.

Though the walls were glass, Will's angle didn't allow him to see who she was ushering inside. He was more caught off guard by the gasp coming from anti-cousins Katie, Charles and Dixon.

"Zoe?" Will asked, focusing back on the door. An

older woman close to his father's age stepped inside. She was tall like a Ravens, with silky gray hair like his grandmother's and almond-shaped eyes like his grandfather Joe's. Blood pounded between his ears. He knew the answer of her identity before Zoe introduced the guest.

"I figured you would want another shareholder here," Zoe said, giving Will a wink. His heart fluttered back to life. "Everyone, in case you didn't realize it, this is your Aunt Octavia."

"How in the hell?" Dixon growled.

"Hello, everyone," Octavia said. Her voice was like a melody. "Katie, how nice to see you again."

"Again?" the pro-cousins cried.

Katie sat back in her seat as her face turned beet red. "I was going to send for you."

"What is going on here?" Marcus asked. He came over and extended his hand to his aunt. "I'm Marcus Ravens, Mark's son."

One by one everyone introduced themselves to their long-lost family member. Will stood off to the side, his arm wrapped around Zoe's waist. "How on Earth did you find her?"

"Actually your cousins did," Zoe beamed. "I overheard them at the pageant a few weeks back. I knew your cousin Katie found your aunt at a nail shop in Pennsylvania."

"I thought you flew to Pennsylvania for an interview at Pink Stiletto Cosmetics in Aston." Will distinctly recalled the trip. It was the first time he'd become nervous about Zoe moving farther away for a job.

"I was," Zoe nodded, "but I recalled the conversation I overheard and went out to find your aunt. When

I heard how your cousins wanted to reintroduce her to the family after a vote had been made, I thought I'd better see if she was interested in coming back and visiting before anything happened to the company."

Will bent down and kissed Zoe. His lips locked with hers and there was no way he wanted to let go. He cupped her face, breaking only to remind her of what he'd said every day since they returned from Southwood. "I love you."

"Uh, it still doesn't matter," Charles began, knocking his knuckles against the tabletop. Everyone surrounding Octavia turned to give him their attention. "No offense, Aunt Octavia, but your generation only acts to advise the board, and we're the board."

"Aunt Octavia's vote still counts," Eva announced as she wrapped her arm around their aunt's shoulders. "Grandma still has her down as a shareholder. Our folks still have their shares, which we control, and we also have shares, as well."

"Be sure to explain how her vote has counted. You know, the abstaining kind," Katie sneered with glee. "Even if she voted, you're still outnumbered since J.J. and Cora have agreed with us."

"You're short," said Brandon.

Spunky as Grandma Naomi, Octavia frowned. "Oh, dear," Octavia's voice dripped with sarcasm. "I worked close with my father. I understand any grandchildren would be given shares at their birth. I'm sure we'll have to get the lawyers in here to double check. But I know it's fact. If you guys want a rough vote right now, I wonder if I can advise my son, Joseph, to vote to keep Ravens Cosmetics running." She tiptoed to the glass door and ushered in the damn-near splitting image of

Donovan, minus the scar. "This is my son, Joseph. I kept him away from the family for a reason and clearly I was wrong. Y'all need each other."

"It's still just one vote," said Katie.

Will began to groan but Zoe patted his back. When he glanced down to read her face, she nodded at the closed doors, which Aunt Octavia opened again.

"Allow me to introduce you all to your other cousins, my twins, Amber and Audra."

"Guess y'all should have done a little more investigating," Eva laughed.

Joyce and Dana both leaned across the table toward Katie. "We outnumber you now."

Whatever bickering went on, Will didn't care. Legally, the pro-cousins had won this round. Will wrapped his arms around Zoe again. "You are my hero, you know that?"

Zoe pressed her lips together and nodded. "Given that I'm a nerd, I'll take that as a compliment."

After the hustle and bustle of New York Fashion week, Zoe was excited to finally get back to Southwood to meet up with her parents to witness their re-proposal. Because of everyone's busy calendars, they kept having to reschedule their vacation. It was a shame Will couldn't make it this weekend, but given the excitement of the return of Octavia Ravens, Ravens Cosmetics was constantly in the news, and that was a good thing. Titus resigned and the position was still open.

"How does she look?" Dressed in a dark suit similar to the one he'd worn over twenty-five years ago, Frank Baldwin met Zoe as she came down the walkway of the backyard of Magnolia Palace.

The "she" would be her mother, Jamerica. "She's beautiful and ready for you to propose again." Zoe added the last bit with a teasing eye roll. She enjoyed her parents involving her with this re-creation. This made her feel more of a family, since they were already so nontraditional. How many children got to witness their parents' engagement? But that was something Zoe had learned over the last few weeks. Family—no matter where they were or how close or far they were from each other—was family.

Last week Zoe had had the time of her life at the Ravens compound celebrating Grandma Naomi Ravens's ninetieth birthday. Away from the company, the anti-cousins were not as intimidating. Octavia was there, along with her three kids, and she shared the reason why she'd left. She'd been too afraid to face her parents. Back then, teen pregnancy was not popular. Either way, Zoe thoroughly enjoyed her time with Will and his family, but she just wished she and Will could have had more time together.

"It's important to create memories, Zoe," her father said, tugging her arm. "Most people like to renew their vows."

"But we're not most people." Zoe nodded and laughed. Her canvas shoes hit the front step of the boards to the dock. The cooling weather called for a long, pumpkin-colored sweater layered over a cream camisole and cuffed denim shorts. She figured she'd take the sweater off after her father proposed. Later on today, Ramon Torres would fire up the grill and Zoe secretly hoped she'd get a chance to see Kenzie once again. With everything going on in her mind, Zoe tripped over the raised wood of the dock.

"My clumsy daughter." Frank chuckled.

"Whatever."

Frank patted Zoe's hand. "Just remember, I'll always be here to catch you."

"Uh, thanks," Zoe said slowly. Her father quit walking and Zoe raised a brow. "What are you doing?"

"I think I forgot the ring," he began, backing up. "Can you do me a favor and make sure your mother doesn't come around that corner and find the spot empty?"

Zoe rolled her eyes. "Fine." How could he have forgotten the important part of the day? Zoe shook her head and laughed at the craziness of her parents. While her father fretted over the ring, her mother was in the bathroom scrutinizing the beauty work Zoe had done on her.

While hurricane season was still in full effect for Florida, Southwood was in line for the powerful weather. The magnolia leaves were gone but the wood of the docks was still slippery. Zoe kept her head down to make sure she didn't slip. Not looking ahead, she nearly walked into an unexpected figure on the dock.

"Whoa, sorry," Zoe exclaimed. Then she locked eyes with Will. "Oh, my God, what are you doing around here?" She threw her arms around his neck. Will spun her around two times before setting her down. She placed her hand against his chest. He still wore a light-blue button-down Oxford shirt with a pair of khakis. "Did you leave work early?"

"Sort of," Will said, visibly gulping.

With her hand still on his shirt, she felt his heartbeat pounding against her palm. "What's wrong? Is someone hurt? Did something happen with your grand-mother?"

"Zoe." Will chuckled and pulled her hands down to her sides. "Everything at home is fine."

"Then what are you doing here?"

"I came…" he began, letting go of her hand. With his fingers he began to unbutton his shirt. "Zoe, since laying eyes on you in Kelly Towers three months ago, you have been an intricate part of my life. You've been my best friend, my confidant and the woman I have fallen in love with."

"Will?" Zoe cocked her head to the side and watched Will get down on one knee. Tears sprang to her eyes. A drop clung to her bottom lash, blinding her. Once she wiped it away, Will had completely taken off his Oxford and underneath he wore a blue cape.

"Zoe, a few months ago you asked me to choose you, and I am down here on bended knee, asking—no—" Will shook his head "—I'm begging you to choose me and be my wife."

"Are you serious?" The words barely got out of her mouth. She couldn't swallow past the lump in her throat. She knelt down with Will and began kissing him without a care in the world for her lipstick.

Will broke the kiss first. His thumbs wiped away the happy tears. "I've never been more serious in my life, Zoe. Please save me one last time and tell me you'll marry me."

All her life Zoe had wanted to be a part of Ravens. Before falling in love with Will, she thought it was the business she wanted to be a part of, but after getting to know everyone, Zoe realized she wanted to be a part of his life and his family. She'd known about their history and now she had the chance to be a part of the future. "Oh, my God, yes, a thousand times over, yes."

"I have this ring," Will said. His hands nervously reached into his pocket. The pear-shaped diamond sparkled in the afternoon sun. It was the ring she'd spied in picture after picture during her research on women marrying into the Ravens family tree. The heirloom was passed on from generation to generation. "It belongs to you, Zoe. You were meant to be a Ravens."

* * * * *

Donovan emptied the last of his drink. "You know what's funny?"

"What?" Chloe asked, finally turning to fully face him.

Chloe blinked and Donovan could have sworn time slackened to slow motion. She fixed her doe eyes directly on him.

"We've known each other since we were kids, attended the same schools and lived within the same social circles for years and there's still a lot I don't know about you."

"You're right," Chloe acknowledged.

"We should do something about that." His desire flew past his lips before he had a chance to filter the thought.

Chloe cleared her throat.

"How about dinner tomorrow night?" *Why waste time?* Donovan thought. He wanted to learn more about Chloe Chandler and he had no intentions of toying with his interest. "I know a beautiful place on the other side of the island."

"That should be fine." Chloe looked at her watch and then looked toward the resort's entrance. "Let me check with Jewel and make sure—"

"Just you and me," Donovan interjected.

"Oh…" Chloe's surprise and coyness made him smile once gain.

"I'm sure Jewel wouldn't mind but do check with her to make sure. I wouldn't want her to feel left out." The fact that Jewel had never returned from her "bathroom" run wasn't lost on him. Jewel was rooting for him and he was sure that she was intentionally giving them space.

"I'll do that." Chloe looked at the door again before sitting back.

"It's been a while. I don't think she's coming back," Donovan responded to Chloe's constant looking back toward the hotel.

"Maybe I should go check on her. She did have quite a few of those rum cocktails."

Donovan stood. "Come on." He held his hand out. "I'll walk you to your suite."

Chloe looked at him for a moment before taking his outstretched hand. A quick current shot through him when their palms touched. Donovan liked it. He wondered if she felt it, too, and if she did, had she enjoyed it as much as he had?

Don't miss IT STARTED IN PARADISE
by Nicki Night, available July 2017
wherever Harlequin® Kimani Romance™
books and ebooks are sold.

Get 2 Free Books,

Plus 2 Free Gifts—

just for trying the Reader Service!

LIT
NOD